Tangled Love

Brianna Owczarzak

Copyright © 2020 Brianna Owczarzak

All rights reserved.

ISBN: 9798663917995

DEDICATION

For my dad, Richard. The strongest and most caring man I will ever know. Thank you for your unwavering support, always.

ACKNOWLEDGMENTS

I want to start by thanking my husband, Ryan. Your support and words of encouragement helped keep me motivated throughout this whole process. I love you.

I also want to thank my dad, Richard, and my sister, Rikki. When I decided to start writing a book, you two believed in me. You were excited to read the book before I even began writing it. Thank you for your continued support.

Finally, I want to thank my friends Amanda, David and Whitney. I entrusted you with the first draft version of this book and your advice and feedback helped shape it. I appreciate you more than you know.

Luca noticed Sarah reading by herself on the beach and introduced himself in Italian, until he learned Sarah was American and then he switched to English. His accent captured Sarah's attention right away. She was always a sucker for a foreign accent.

Luca wasn't bad on the eyes either. He was 6'1" and had the muscles of a swimmer. He had dark brown hair and eyes that shined like copper. Sarah was instantly attracted to him and that attraction was mutual because Luca asked Sarah to accompany him on a date. She of course said yes because that was why she was in Italy in the first place. Images from the movie *Taken* flashed briefly through her head, but she had Luca agree to meet her at a public place.

Sarah was strolling through the narrow streets of Vernazza the next day, looking for the restaurant they were scheduled to meet at. She was about to ask for directions when she saw Luca waving to her. He was standing near a small table outside the restaurant. She walked up to him with a smile and he greeted her with a kiss on each cheek.

"Ciao bella," Luca said. "You made it."

"I did," Sarah replied, still smiling.

"I got us this table outside. Please, take a seat," Luca said, pulling out a chair for Sarah.

Sarah sat down at the table and looked around. The buildings surrounding them were different shades of red, yellow, and orange. Some of the buildings were a little run down, but they were still beautiful. She looked across the table at Luca who was examining her.

"It's beautiful," she said.

"Yes, you are," Luca said.

Sarah blushed. She didn't know if Luca misunderstood her or if he was being cute. He smiled at her.

"What brings you to Italy, Sarah?" Luca asked.

Sarah loved the way her name sounded coming from Luca's lips.

"Adventure. Culture. The food. I love everything about Italy. I'm so envious of the people who get to live here. Everything is so beautiful," Sarah replied.

"I'm sure America is beautiful too," Luca said.

"No," Sarah said laughing. "We don't have the history or architecture you have over here."

"But you have Hollywood," Luca said excitedly.

Sarah laughed. She knew Hollywood wasn't all glitz and glamour like it's made up to be, but she wasn't about to explain that to Luca. She just nodded her head in agreement. She was about to start looking at the menu when her cell phone began vibrating. She looked at the screen and saw it was her Aunt Susan calling. Sarah wasn't really close with her aunt, but Susan was the only family she had besides her dad.

"I'm sorry, I have to take this," Sarah said.

Sarah stood up from the table and walked a few steps away before she answered her phone.

"Hey, Aunt Susan," Sarah said.

Sarah's mouth quickly dropped. Her aunt had called to tell Sarah her dad, Edward Simmons, had fallen ill. He was just diagnosed with stage four lung cancer and it wasn't looking good. After hanging up the phone, Sarah walked back to the table.

"I'm so sorry Luca, but I have to go," Sarah said.

"But we haven't ordered our food yet," Luca said confused.

"I know. I'm sorry. It was really nice to meet you," she said, holding back tears.

She quickly walked away before Luca could see her cry. She rushed back to her hotel room and searched for a return flight home. She was supposed to stay in Italy another week, but she knew she had to get home to her dad.

There wasn't a flight available until the next day. She sat in her room replaying the news in her head. Lung cancer. It didn't make sense. Her dad had never smoked a day in his life. It must have been all of the time he spent inside casinos, Sarah thought to herself.

Edward loved to gamble. It was something about the luck of the draw on the blackjack table that made his heart pump. It wasn't just blackjack though, he would play everything from slots, to craps, to even bingo. He would go to the casino three to four times a week. Sarah knew he had a problem, but he won enough times where it never became a financial issue. So she just let him have his fun. Now his love of gambling was catching up to him, Sarah thought.

The next day, Sarah flew back home to her dad. She was living with him at the time because it didn't make much sense to pay for an apartment while she was off traveling. Upon returning home, Sarah learned her dad's cancer was aggressive. He started treatment immediately, which included five radiation treatments every week.

Sarah knew she had to get a job to help out financially. Prior to that point, she had only been working odd jobs here and there to save up enough money for her next adventure. But with her dad needing so much care, Sarah knew she had to help out.

She noticed a bookstore on Main Street in downtown Muncie was looking for a manager. It wasn't much, but it would help pay the bills, Sarah thought. She applied for the position. Her knowledge of foreign places and cultures suited her well for the job and she was hired on the spot.

The bookstore allowed Sarah to work flexible hours so she could help take her dad to his doctor's appointments. Watching her dad fight such a brutal disease was hard for Sarah. He was the strongest man she had ever known.

Edward was drafted into the Vietnam War in 1969 at the age of 22. He had been working at the Chevrolet plant in Muncie at the time. But when the duty called, he quit his job to serve his country. He considered himself lucky to make it out of the war alive, because he knew several people who didn't. He didn't like to talk about his time in the service much, but in Sarah's eyes, he was a hero. When he returned home, he went back to work at the plant. He worked there until the plant shut down in 2006, forcing him to retire.

Eight years after retirement is when he was diagnosed with cancer. The prognosis wasn't good, but Sarah believed with all her heart her dad could get through it. He had to get through it. He was the only man she had ever loved. When Sarah wasn't working or taking her dad to his treatments, she was researching different things that could help him get better. She tried changing his diet, but Edward was a stubborn man. He liked what he liked and that was that. She also tried to get him active, but again, he was stubborn. He hadn't exercised in 20 some years and he wasn't going to start then.

One Wednesday, about three weeks after her dad started his treatments, Sarah was sitting in the waiting room with him when a young male nurse walked in. He must be new, she thought, because she had never seen him there before. He was tall, but not too tall. About 5'11" if she had to guess. He had sandy blonde hair and piercing blue eyes. He was quite attractive and Sarah couldn't pull her eyes away from him, even though she knew it wasn't polite to stare.

"Hey Tim," Edward said as the man walked towards him and Sarah.

Sarah, in disbelief that her father knew this beautiful creature, broke her focus from the male nurse and was looking at her dad confused.

"Good morning, Mr. Simmons. How are you feeling today?" the man asked Edward.

Sarah looked back at the man, who must be Tim.

"Oh, the usual. Say, were you able to bring me any of those donuts you were talking about last time?" Edward asked Tim.

"Now Mr. Simmons, you know you shouldn't be eating sweets," Tim replied.

Tim turned his attention to Sarah, who was still examining him – wondering why she never noticed him before.

"Can't you do anything about his diet?" Tim asked Sarah jokingly.

Sarah let out a laugh.

"I've tried, but this old man is stuck in his ways," Sarah replied. "I'm Sarah, by the way," she said as she extended her hand.

"Nice to meet you, Sarah. My name is Tim and I'm one of the nurses on your father's medical team," Tim responded, while shaking her hand.

Sarah noticed Tim wasn't wearing a wedding ring. Maybe he's single, she thought, or maybe it's against protocol to wear jewelry.

"How long have you been working with my dad?" Sarah asked.

"About a week now," Tim replied. "I recently transferred here from another center."

"Tim is one of the better ones," Edward butted in. "He doesn't give me that bullshit spiel about exercise."

"Dad!" Sarah said embarrassed.

"Oh hush. Like Tim has never heard a curse word before," Edward replied.

Edward's language was rather colorful after working 40 years in an automobile plant.

"It's OK, Sarah," Tim said while laughing. "I'm getting used to your dad's vocabulary."

Sarah looked down at the floor.

"Well, Mr. Simmons. Let's take you back there so you can get out of here," Tim said.

"Sounds good to me," Edward replied.

Edward stood up and followed Tim to the back room where they perform the treatments.

That was the first time Sarah met Tim. The exchange was brief and nothing note-worthy happened, but for some reason she couldn't get him out of her head. After that day, Sarah looked forward to taking her dad to his treatments. She volunteered to take him to all of them, even though he insisted she didn't have to. She changed her schedule at the bookstore so she only worked in the evenings. That freed her up to take her dad to his appointments every Monday through Friday, which also meant more Tim time.

During their visits to the cancer treatment center, Sarah would strike up small talk with Tim to try to learn more about him. She learned he grew up in Kalamazoo, Michigan, received his bachelor's degree from Ball State University, and fell in love with Muncie that he chose to stay. His favorite color was blue, he loved Thai food, and he recently took up fishing. Since she was contained to the waiting room, there weren't a lot of opportunities to get to know Tim. But that didn't stop her from trying.

"Hey Tim, you seeing anybody?" Edward asked Tim during one of his treatments.

This was on a Wednesday, two weeks after Sarah and Tim's first initial conversation. Sarah immediately looked at her dad. She hadn't mentioned anything about her infatuation to Tim to him, so she didn't know where this was coming from. And Edward was never one to meddle with Sarah's love life. As far as Sarah knew, her dad preferred if she didn't have one.

"No sir, not at the moment. But I'm sorry to break it to you, you're not quite my type," Tim responded jokingly.

Edward and Sarah both let out a laugh.

"I knew you weren't queer," Edward said.

Sarah put her face in her hands. Tim let out a laugh. Sarah picked her head back up with a slight smile.

"I was wondering when you were going to quit diddle-dallying around and ask my daughter out?" Edward asked.

"Dad!" Sarah exclaimed, not believing what was happening.

"What? I've been watching you two beat around the bush for two weeks now. Just go out already," Edward said.

"Oh my God," Sarah said as she put her face back in her hands.

"I wouldn't be opposed to that," Tim said, finally joining the conversation.

Sarah looked up at him.

"What?" she asked, surprised.

"I would love to take you out," Tim responded.

Sarah smiled.

"Alright, now that that's over with. Let's get my treatment out of the way and you two love birds can work out the details after," Edward said, pleased with himself.

Edward and Tim walked back to the treatment room, but before the door closed, Tim turned back towards Sarah and gave her a wink. She blushed and her heart was racing. It had been a while since Sarah had a crush on somebody. There was Luca a few weeks prior, but that was just a brief encounter. She didn't even get to enjoy their date.

Sarah wasn't thinking about Luca anymore or what could have been. She was thinking about Tim and she liked where this was headed. About 15 minutes later, Edward and Tim entered the waiting room. Normally, it would have just been Edward, but Sarah and Tim had a date to plan.

"I'll uh, grab my coat," Edward said as he walked over to the coat rack.

Sarah smiled as she stood up and approached Tim.

"Sorry about my dad," she said embarrassed.

"No, I'm glad he said something," Tim said smiling. "So what are you doing on Saturday?"

Sarah put her finger on her chin as she pretended to think.

"I think I could free up some time," she said. "What did you have in mind?"

"Well, I know this great Thai restaurant on Main Street," Tim said.

"Tuppee Tong?" Sarah asked. "That's right by my work. I know exactly where that is."

"So it's a date?" Tim asked.

"It's a date," Sarah confirmed. "I'll meet you there around 7?"

"That sounds perfect," Tim said.

Sarah smiled and gave Tim a wave, as she went to meet her dad at the door.

"Wait," Tim said.

Sarah turned back around.

"Yes?" she asked.

"We should probably exchange phone numbers in case anything happens," Tim said shyly.

"Ah, smart thinking," Sarah said with a smile.

She walked back towards Tim and pulled out her cell phone. They exchanged phone numbers. Then Sarah left the office with her dad.

"You're welcome," Edward said with a smirk as they walked towards Sarah's car.

"How did you know?" Sarah asked.

"Darlin', I know I'm interesting, but I'm not that interesting where you want to spend every day with me. I knew something was up when you changed your schedule around and it didn't take me long to realize it was that handsome feller in there," Edward responded.

"Dad," Sarah said as she gave her dad a friendly push.

That night, Sarah received a text message from Tim. Is he canceling already, she thought to herself before she opened the text.

Hey. I just wanted to make sure you didn't give me a fake number out of pity, the text read.

He texted in complete sentences. Sarah liked that.

Haha, no. This is my real number, Sarah replied.

Good. I can't wait for Saturday, Tim texted back.

Me either. Have a good night, Sarah responded.

You too, Tim replied.

That night, Sarah went to bed with a smile on her face. The next morning she arranged for her aunt to take Edward to his appointment. She was excited, giddy even, about seeing Tim. But she didn't want to say anything that would make him want to cancel their date on Saturday. She figured it would be best if she waited until the date to see him again. She wondered where this insecurity was coming from. Sarah wasn't an insecure person. She was usually the type of person who went after what she wanted, but Tim was different.

That afternoon, she was sorting books at work. It was her favorite activity to keep her mind off of everything that was happening with her dad's illness and her insecurities about her upcoming date. It was an easy task, but it required a lot of focus to make sure all of the books were placed in their designated category. Her phone let out a little ping, alerting her she had a text message. She pulled her phone out of her back pocket and saw the message was from Tim.

I missed you today, the text read.

She smiled and leaned up against the bookshelf she was arranging. One day and he's already missing me, Sarah thought to herself. *I missed you too*, she typed, before deleting it and composing a new message. I need to be more mysterious, she thought to herself.

Oh really? she responded.

Yeah, I've been enjoying our daily conversations, he replied.

Me too, but I'll be back tomorrow, Sarah texted.

I'm looking forward to it, Tim responded.

That's it, she decided, no more hiding out. She wanted to see Tim and she was going to see him. She texted her dad and told him she would be taking him to his appointment on Friday. Edward responded to Sarah's message with a gif of an eyeroll.

The next day, Sarah sat in the waiting room with her dad.

"You know, I never would have butted in if I knew this whole dating thing was going to turn you into a weirdo," Edward said.

"What are you talking about?" Sarah asked offended.

"You changed your outfit three times today to drive me to my doctor's appointment," Edward said, giving his daughter a stern look.

"Dad!" Sarah exclaimed.

The door opened and Tim walked into the waiting room.

"How's my favorite patient doing today?" Tim asked Edward before flashing Sarah a smile.

Sarah gave Edward a glare that said, "You better not say anything."

"Well, you know what they say, it's a great day for the race," Edward said.

"What race?" Tim asked.

"The human race," Edward said, giving his daughter a wink.

Edward stood up and made his way towards the door to receive his treatment.

"I'll, uh, see you tomorrow," Sarah told Tim.

"I'm looking forward to it," he replied, before entering the door with Edward.

2

When Saturday rolled around, Sarah was full of emotions. She was excited about her date with Tim, but at the same time, she felt bad she was going out and having fun while her dad sat at home. She knew she should be spending as much time with him as possible, but he was the one who insisted on this date. He basically set it up. She pushed those thoughts out of her mind and focused on getting ready. What to wear, she thought to herself. It was only dinner, but that doesn't mean it won't turn into something afterwards, she thought.

    Sarah wasn't the type of woman who had sex on the first date. Especially with someone she was going to have to see nearly every day for the next two weeks – that's how long her dad's first round of radiation was scheduled for. She settled on a simple summer dress – classy and cute – and a light cardigan in case she were to get cold. Even though it was June, the temperatures tended to dip when the sun went down. The next wardrobe debate was heels or flats. Being only 5'4", she chose heels. That way if the night ended with a kiss, Tim wouldn't have to lean too far down to reach her lips – which were perfectly coated with cherry-flavored lip gloss.

Sarah drove herself downtown and parked her car right outside the bookshop, which was two blocks down the street from the Thai restaurant they were meeting at. If Tim offered to walk her back to her car after dinner, it gave them a few more minutes together, she thought. She pulled down her visor to check her hair and make-up in the mirror. That'll do, she thought. She exited her car and walked the two blocks to Tuppee Tong, where Tim was waiting for her outside. He was wearing khakis, a blue and white plaid button-down shirt, and a navy sports coat. He cleans up good, Sarah thought to herself.

"Hey there, beautiful," Tim said to her.

"Hey," Sarah said with a nervous laugh, trying to think back to when her last date was.

She briefly thought about Luca, but quickly pushed him out of her head.

"Shall we?" Tim asked as he put his arm out towards her.

"We shall," she replied, taking his arm.

The two walked into the restaurant, arm in arm.

"Hi, we have a reservation under Conner," Tim told the hostess.

His last name is Conner, Sarah noted to herself, realizing she had no idea what his last name was prior to that moment.

"Right this way, Mr. Conner," the hostess replied, taking Sarah and Tim to their table.

Tim held Sarah's chair out for her and helped scoot her closer to the table before taking his own seat.

"Such a gentleman," Sarah said.

"It's that good 'ol Midwestern hospitality," Tim replied with a smile.

"So your last name is Conner?" Sarah asked.

"Yup. It used to be O'Conner, but the O was stripped away when my great-grandparents emigrated here from Ireland," he said.

"Ah, a good 'ol Irish lad," Sarah said with a laugh.

"What about you? What's your family's heritage?" Tim asked.

"Well, my great-grandparents on my dad's side came here from Cornwall. But I'm not sure where my mom's ancestors were from," Sarah responded.

"So it's just you and your dad?" Tim asked.

"Yeah, my mom passed away in a car accident when I was about 5-years-old," Sarah said.

"I'm so sorry to hear that," Tim replied, grabbing Sarah's hand lightly.

"It's OK. That was a while ago," she said, giving him a smile.

Tim lifted her hand and kissed it ever so lightly. Sarah blushed and pulled her hand back so she could look at the menu.

"What do you recommend?" she asked while scanning the menu.

"If you like seafood, the pad Phuket is delicious. But if you're in the mood for chicken, you can't go wrong with the lemon grass chicken," Tim replied.

"Ooh, that lemon grass chicken does sound good. I think I'll go with that," Sarah said while reading the description.

A waiter walked over to the table.

"Are you two ready to order?" he asked.

"Yes, we will both have the lemon grass chicken," Tim told the waiter before turning to Sarah. "Would you like anything to drink?"

"I'm fine with water," she replied.

Turning his attention back to the waiter, "We'll just have those two entrees, please."

"I'll put that in right away," the waiter said before walking away.

"So what's your story, Miss Simmons? What do you like to do for fun?" Tim asked.

"My story? Well, once upon a time there was a beautiful princess," Sarah said laughing.

Tim smiled.

"For fun, I enjoy traveling, hiking, anything adventurous really," she said.

"If you could go anywhere, where would it be?" Tim asked.

"Ironically, I would love to go to Thailand," Sarah said while looking around the restaurant.

Tim, pretending to take notes in an invisible notebook, said, "Take Sarah to Thailand."

Sarah laughed.

"What are you doing?" she asked.

"Taking notes for our next date," Tim replied.

"Oh, so you just assume there's going to be a second date?" Sarah asked with a grin.

"I'm hopeful," Tim replied, returning the smile.

"Well, if that second date is a trip to Thailand, how can I say no?" Sarah asked.

Tim laughed.

The waiter returned with their food. They ate, laughed, and shared more stories with one another.

Sarah learned Tim had two older brothers, had never been outside of the United States, and had a heart-shaped scar on his knee from an injury while playing baseball in high school. Tim learned about Sarah's many world adventures, her love of books, and her competitive nature when it comes to board games.

The waiter cleared the table and asked the two if they saved any room for dessert. Tim looked at Sarah who shook her head no.

"I'll just take the bill, please," Tim told the waiter.

"No problem," the waiter responded before leaving the table.

"I had a lot of fun," Sarah said, smiling at Tim.

"Me too," Tim responded. "So what's next?"

"What do you mean?" Sarah asked confused.

"I mean, the night is young. What do you want to do next?" Tim asked.

"I have an idea," Sarah said with a grin.

The waiter returned with the bill. Tim pulled out his wallet, placed some cash inside the slot and told the waiter it was all set. Tim and Sarah left the restaurant.

"Thanks for dinner," Sarah said as they walked outside.

"You're quite welcome," Tim said, grabbing her hand. "So where to, my lady?"

"This way," Sarah said, leading him down the road towards her car. "I want to show you something."

They walked the two blocks to the bookshop, where Sarah stopped. She pulled the keys to the store out from her purse and unlocked the door, leading Tim inside. She closed the door behind him and locked it so no one else could come in. After all, the store was closed.

"This is where I work," Sarah said, motioning around the store. "All of these books are just adventures waiting to be read."

"It's impressive," Tim said looking around.

"It's a bookstore," Sarah said with a laugh. "But this is my happy place."

"We serve coffee over there," she said pointing to the corner with a chalkboard menu. "And up here," she said, taking Tim's hand and leading him to the stairs, "is my favorite place in the whole store."

Sarah and Tim walked up the stairs holding hands. At the top, there were rows and rows of bookshelves lined with vintage books. In the middle of the room was a big orange couch, two wingback chairs, and a coffee table. Sarah led Tim over to the couch.

"This is the most comfortable couch in the whole world," Sarah exclaimed, sitting down.

Tim took a seat on the couch next to her.

"It is pretty comfortable," he said, leaning back. "But it's not as comfortable as my couch," he said, putting his arm around Sarah.

"I guess I'll have to be the judge of that," she said, snuggling into him with her head on his chest.

Tim looked down at her. She looked up at him. He pulled her chin up lightly with his fingers and stared into her brown eyes for a second before their lips met. They kissed once and didn't pull away. Tim moved his right hand behind her neck and kissed her more passionately. His lips pulled on her upper lip for a second before releasing. His tongue entered her mouth. Her tongue entered his. Tim slowly removed her cardigan and Sarah took off his sport coat.

She climbed on top of him with her legs straddling his. She began unbuttoning his shirt while kissing his neck. Tim grabbed her lower earlobe with his lips and gave it a little nibble. Sarah let out a soft moan. She opened her eyes, realizing where they were. She sat up, still holding his partially unbuttoned shirt in her hands. She bit her lower lip and looked Tim in the eyes.

"We shouldn't be doing this," she said. "Not here. Not now."

Tim removed his hands from Sarah's waist and placed them on either side of him.

"But it was fun," he said with a smile.

Sarah laughed and rolled off of him.

"Yes it was," she said.

They sat on the couch for a moment catching their breath. Sarah leaned in and gave Tim a kiss on his cheek. He turned his head toward her and gave her a light kiss on the lips.

"Are you ready, sir?" she asked.

"I guess," he replied with a shrug.

They stood up and Sarah went to walk towards the stairs, but Tim grabbed her hand and pulled her back. He wrapped her up in a hug.

"Thank you for a great night," he whispered in her ear.

Still hugging, she looked up at him and said, "You're quite welcome."

He leaned down and kissed her again. Their lips stayed locked for a moment before they both pulled away. Their eyes met and they gave each other a smile.

"Alright, let's go," Tim said reluctantly.

The pair walked hand in hand down the stairs. They walked towards the door, but Tim stopped.

Looking around, he said, "I'll have to come and see this place during the day sometime."

"But I think I'm going to prefer the night version," he said, giving Sarah a wink.

She laughed. They walked out of the store and Sarah locked it back up.

"Well, this is my car," Sarah said, pointing at her car. "Do you need a ride to yours?"

"No, I'm just up the street," Tim replied.

He grabbed both of her hands with his and held them to his lips.

"When can I see you again?" he asked.

"I'm sure I'll see you Monday," she said with a wink.

"You know what I mean," he insisted.

"When do you want to?" Sarah asked.

"How about tomorrow?" Tim replied.

She laughed and let go of his hands. She walked towards her car.

"Pick me up for coffee. I'll text you my address," she said.

Sarah entered her car and drove home. She was wondering if her dad was going to interrogate her about their date, but he was already asleep. Sarah went upstairs to her bedroom and texted Tim her address for their coffee date. She laid on her bed with the biggest smile on her face. She fell asleep dreaming of that passionate kiss, and what would have happened if she didn't put the brakes on.

3

The morning after her date with Tim, Sarah went downstairs to make her and her dad some breakfast. She found him hunched over the kitchen table struggling to catch his breath.

"Dad, are you OK?" she asked concerned.

Edward looked up at her with pain in his eyes.

"I'm just having one of those days," he replied.

With his cancer treatments, Edward had good days and he had bad days. The good days outweighed the bad, but when the bad days arrived, they were rough. They usually didn't require any medical treatment and could be treated at home with rest and lots of fluids, but it didn't make it any easier for Sarah to see her dad that way. She immediately texted Tim and told him they would have to reschedule because her dad wasn't feeling well. He responded that he understood and to give Edward his best. Sarah helped her dad make his way to the couch where she covered him up with a blanket and turned the TV on for him.

He looked tired, she thought. A lifetime of battles was catching up to him. He had bags under his eyes from decades of not receiving enough sleep. Some things are never the same after you've been in a war, and sleep is one of them. Sarah didn't know what her dad experienced when he was in the service. He would only ever say, "Some things you can't unsee." She knew he had a hard time sleeping at night, even all these years later.

"Do you want me to get you anything?" she asked him.

"I'm fine," he responded.

"You know, you really should eat something," Sarah insisted.

"I'm not hungry," he replied grumpily.

"OK, well I'll be right here if you need anything," Sarah said, sitting down in a chair next to the couch.

About a half hour later, the doorbell rang, awaking Edward from his short nap. Sarah got up out of the chair and went and answered the door. It was Tim. He had a brown paper bag in one hand and a tray of hot beverages in the other.

"Hi," Sarah said surprised.

"You said your dad wasn't feeling well so I figured I would bring him some chicken noodle soup," Tim said, holding up the brown paper bag.

"And I also thought maybe we could move our coffee date here," he said, nodding his head towards the beverages.

"Who is it?" Edward yelled raspily from the living room.

"It's Tim," Sarah responded, turning her head in her father's direction.

"Well don't just stand there, invite the man in," Edward said, sitting up on the couch.

Sarah looked back at Tim and smiled.

"Come on in," she said, stepping aside to allow room for him to enter.

Tim walked into the home and began looking around when he saw Edward.

"Good morning, Mr. Simmons. I brought you some soup to help you feel better," Tim said, holding up the brown paper bag.

"Oh good, I'm starving," Edward replied.

Sarah's mouth dropped a little, but she stopped herself from saying anything.

"I'll fix him a bowl if you want to make yourself comfortable," she said, taking the brown paper bag from Tim.

Sarah carried the bag into the kitchen where she prepared a bowl for her dad. Tim walked over to the couch and handed Edward one of the beverages.

"Here, sir. I brought you some hot tea. It should help open up your lungs and make it easier for you to breathe," he said.

Edward took the cup from Tim, eyeing him suspiciously.

"What's your objective here?" Edward asked him.

Tim laughed.

"No objective, sir. I wanted to see your daughter again and I thought you would like some hot soup and tea," he replied with a smile.

"I'll allow it. Please, have a seat," Edward said, motioning towards the chair Sarah was sitting in.

Sarah returned to the living room with the bowl of soup and handed it to her father.

"Be careful, it's hot," she said.

She looked over at Tim with a smile, wondering how someone so attractive could be so kind. Sarah was used to one or the other, but not both characteristics. She thought something must be wrong with him, no one can be that perfect. But she quickly pushed that thought aside and focused on the present. She had this beautiful man in her house, helping care for her father.

"Here, this is for you," Tim said, handing Sarah a coffee.

"Thank you," Sarah said, taking the cup. "Would you like to go sit in the kitchen?"

"Sure," Tim said, standing up from the chair. "After you," he motioned.

Sarah gave her dad a kiss on the forehead.

"Let me know if you need anything, dad. We'll be right in here," she said, nodding towards the kitchen.

Sarah led Tim to the kitchen where they both placed their coffee cups on the table. He grabbed her hand and pulled her into a hug.

"How are you?" he asked softly in her ear.

Holding him close, she let out a sigh and replied, "I've been better."

"I know days like this can be rough, that's why I wanted to help in any way I could," he said. "If I'm overstepping in any way, please let me know and I'll leave."

Sarah looked up at Tim with a confused look on her face.

"You're not overstepping. I am happy to have the help. I couldn't get him to eat or drink anything before you got here. So thank you," she said, standing on her tiptoes to give him a kiss.

Sarah wanted to push Tim up against her refrigerator and kiss him like the night before, but she refrained from doing so. Instead, she pulled away quickly and gave him a smile. Tim returned the smile and pressed his lips to her forehead.

"So, this is your house," Tim said, looking around.

"Yup. I've lived here my whole life," she said. "Do you want a tour?"

"Sure," Tim replied.

"Well, obviously, this is the kitchen. And back there," Sarah said, motioning toward a room off the kitchen, "is the laundry room."

She led Tim back into the living room, which was adjacent to the kitchen, pointing out a small bathroom on the way.

"I'm going to give Tim a tour of the house. Are you all set?" she asked her dad.

"I'm good," Edward responded.

"This is some good soup," he said to Tim, taking another bite.

"I'm glad you're enjoying it, sir," Tim replied.

Sarah led Tim towards the front door. She pointed to a room on the opposite side of the door from the living room and told him that was the office. Then she led him upstairs to the bedrooms and another bathroom.

"So this must be your room?" Tim asked, opening the door to the only room he hadn't seen.

"Yup. This is where all of my adventures are planned," she said, leading Tim inside.

Her walls were covered with world maps and pictures of the places she had been. She had a vinyl decal on one wall that read "Not all who wander are lost."

"I like that," Tim said, pointing towards the decal.

"Thanks," she said, looking around to make sure there wasn't anything embarrassing laying around.

She noticed a bra hanging on the back of her doorknob. She quickly grabbed it and threw it under her bed while Tim was occupied looking at the photos on her wall.

"You really have been everywhere," he noted.

"Not everywhere. There are still a lot of places I'd love to see," Sarah said, moving next to Tim.

"This was my last trip," she said, pointing to a photo of her on a beach in Italy. "That's where I was when I got the call about my dad."

Tim didn't say anything. He just wrapped his arm around her waist and gave her a little squeeze. Sarah looked up at him with a smile. She was happy he was there. Tim returned the smile before taking a few steps around the room.

"You have Battleship? That was my favorite board game growing up," Tim said, admiring her game collection.

Sarah laughed and moved towards Tim.

"I have a lot of games," she said. "Probably more than a 26-year-old should have."

"Do you want to play a round?" he asked with an excited grin.

"Are you sure you're ready to see my competitive side?" Sarah asked with a smile.

"Bring it on," Tim said.

Sarah grabbed Battleship off of the shelf and moved towards her bed.

"We can play here," she said, taking a seat on the bed.

Tim moved around to the other side of the bed and sat on the edge. He opened the box and began organizing the pieces. Sarah looked at him with a smile and thought to herself, are we really about to play Battleship on my bed?

"Do you remember how to play or do you need a refresher?" Sarah asked Tim.

"Oh, I'm good. Prepare to have your entire naval class defeated," Tim responded with a smile.

The two set up their ships and took turns taking shots at the other player's board. There were a lot of laughs and playful banter back and forth. Towards the end, they both had one ship remaining. Sarah had her battleship, which required four hits to take down, and Tim had his submarine, which required three hits. Tim launched an attack and hit her battleship. She fired back, but missed. Tim launched again, another hit. Sarah returned fire and hit his submarine. They both were two hits away from winning the game.

"No!" Tim exclaimed, before firing.

It was another hit. Sarah fired back, but it was a miss.

"Damnit," she said.

"I've got you now," Tim said with a smile.

Tim launched his final attack. It was a direct hit. Sarah's last ship was defeated and Tim won the game.

"Yes!" Tim said, jumping off the bed with his fists in the air.

Sarah, a little defeated but happy to have found someone as competitive as her, grabbed a pillow from her bed, stood up on her knees and hit Tim with it.

"That's what you get," she said laughing.

"That's how you want to play?" Tim asked, laughing.

He grabbed the pillow from Sarah, climbed back on the bed and hit her with the pillow. She fell back on her back laughing. Tim climbed over her and hit her again with the pillow. Sarah grabbed another pillow and used it as a shield. Tim grabbed that pillow and tossed it aside. They both stared into each other's eyes before he leaned down and kissed her. He dropped the pillow at his side and moved his hands to her neck. He grabbed her lower lip with his teeth and gave it a playful pull before releasing.

Sarah rolled Tim over on his back and climbed on top of him. She forced her lips against his, pushing her tongue inside his mouth. Tim wrapped his arms around her back, while returning the kiss. They made out like that for a few minutes before Tim pulled his head back.

"I should probably go," he said with a smile.

"I don't want you to," Sarah whined.

Tim let out a laugh and gently lifted Sarah to his side. He sat up on the bed, looked Sarah in her eyes and gave her a light kiss on the lips.

"Trust me. I'm enjoying this just as much as you are. But your dad is downstairs and I'm not comfortable taking this any further here," Tim said with a half-smile.

Sarah let out a laugh. Tim looked confused.

"Jesus, Tim. I wasn't going to bang you with my dad downstairs," she said laughing, while giving Tim a playful push.

"Oh, good. I can stay then," Tim said, laying back on the bed with a smile.

Sarah laid down next to him and nuzzled her head into his chest.

"Besides, this is only our second date. I'm not that easy," she said laughing.

"I never meant to imply you were easy," Tim said seriously, lifting Sarah's face to look at him. "I know this is only our second date, but for me it feels like I've known you forever. Maybe that's crazy because we've only known each other a few weeks, but I feel like I know you, Sarah Simmons."

Sarah smiled at Tim.

"I feel the same way," she said.

They both leaned it for a kiss and let their lips meet for a few seconds before pulling back.

"We should probably go check on my dad though to make sure he is OK," Sarah said.

"OK, but you might want to fix your hair," Tim said playfully. "I don't want your dad to get the wrong idea about me."

Sarah looked over at her mirror. Her hair was all over the place from the pillow fight and the makeout session.

"Oh my God!" she exclaimed, jumping off the bed and running towards her desk.

She grabbed her hairbrush and brushed her hair back into place. Tim laughed.

"I thought it was cute," he said.

"Let's go," she said laughing.

The two walked downstairs where they found Edward sound asleep on the couch.

"Are you hungry? I could fix us some lunch," Sarah said to Tim.

Tim looked down at his watch.

"I should probably get going. I have some errands I have to run today," he said.

"Alright, I'll walk you out," Sarah said, a little sad their day was coming to an end.

Sarah led Tim to the front door and walked outside with him. The two of them stood on the porch looking at each other. He grabbed her hands and swung them back and forth a little bit.

"I'm really glad you stopped by," Sarah said with a smile.

"I am too," Tim replied.

He pulled Sarah into a hug and kissed the top of her head. She pulled away and looked up at him with a smile. He leaned down and kissed her on the lips, held his lips there for a couple seconds and slowly released.

"Until next time, Miss Simmons," he said, before turning and walking away.

Sarah watched him get into his car and drive away. She went back into the house and made herself something to eat.

4

Tim was not at Edward's appointment on Monday. It was a woman nurse who greeted Edward in the waiting area and took him back into the treatment room. Tim had been there every day since his transfer. Sarah didn't receive a text from him saying he wasn't going to be there, so she began to worry about him. After she returned home with her dad, she went up to her room to get ready for work.

I missed you today, she began to text Tim before quickly deleting the message. No, she thought, I'll wait for him to text me. She went to work and didn't hear from Tim at all that day. She knew he wasn't obligated to text her, but she had gotten use to talking to him every day. Sarah began to wonder what she did the day before that would cause him to go silent. Or what if something happened to him, she wondered concerned.

The next day, as she was getting ready to take her dad to his appointment, she received a call from the bookstore. They had received a huge shipment of books a few days early and one of the other employees had called out sick. They needed Sarah to head in immediately to help out. Edward arranged for his sister to take him to his appointment. Sarah was bummed she wasn't going to be able to see Tim for a second day, but knew she had to go to work.

"Let me know how it goes," she said to her dad as she was walking out the door.

"You mean, if lover boy is back today," Edward said with a smirk.

Sarah gave her dad a smile and went to work. She put all of her focus into her work so she didn't drive herself crazy thinking about Tim and why he never texted her. She was unloading the boxes of new books that had just arrived when one of her coworkers approached her.

"Hey, Sarah," Cindy said smiling.

Cindy was a 19-year-old Ball State student who worked at the bookstore part-time around her classes. She thought Sarah was so fascinating because she had traveled to so many places. Meanwhile, Cindy had never left Indiana. On the other hand, Sarah found Cindy annoying. She didn't know why, but this girl – who wasn't much younger than her – seemed so blah to her.

"What is it, Cindy?" Sarah asked, trying not to sound annoyed.

"There's a cute guy here asking for you," Cindy said with a huge grin.

Sarah stopped what she was doing. It must be Tim, she thought to herself.

"Where is he?" Sarah asked.

"He's upstairs," Cindy said, pointing up the stairs.

Sarah looked at her reflection in one of the windows. She brushed her hair really quick with her fingers and walked up the stairs. *I can't believe he surprised me at work,* she thought to herself while walking up the stairs. She got to the top of the stairs and looked around. She didn't see Tim anywhere.

"Sarah!" a man exclaimed, quickly approaching her.

"Charlie?" Sarah asked surprised.

"I'm back," Charlie said, picking Sarah up and swinging her around.

Charlie was Sarah's childhood best friend. They were practically inseparable all throughout grade school. They were even each other's date to their senior prom. Everyone, including the two of them, always assumed they would get married. They never dated though. But they did share one romantic kiss before Charlie left for the Air Force after graduation. Since then, Sarah had only seen him a few times and the last time was about two years ago. But they stayed in contact through letters and social media.

"I can't believe you're here," she said, hugging him tight.

"I know. I finally busted out," Charlie said laughing.

"Why didn't you tell me you were coming home?" Sarah asked, pulling away from the hug.

"I wanted to surprise you," he replied.

"You look good. I mean, really good," Sarah said, eying his muscles.

Charlie was 6'2" and 220 pounds of solid muscle. He had dark brown hair and forest green eyes.

"You look good too," he said, putting Sarah in a headlock and rubbing his knuckles on her head.

"Charlie!" she shouted while trying to get away.

"Come sit down and talk to me. What have you been up to?" Charlie asked, leading her over to the couch.

Sarah and Charlie sat on the couch and talked. It was like no time had passed since they last saw each other. They shared stories of their adventures and laughed at some of their old memories - like the time they stole Edward's truck in the middle of the night to watch a meteor shower and ended up getting it suck in the mud.

"What is your dad up to nowadays?" Charlie asked.

Sarah paused, just realizing Charlie didn't know.

"It's not good, Charlie," she said.

"Oh no. What is it?" he asked, putting his hand on her knee.

"He was diagnosed with cancer a little over a month ago. Stage four. It's aggressive," she said. "He's been receiving radiation treatments, but I don't know if it's working. He just seems so weak and tired these days."

"I'm so sorry, Sarah," Charlie said, hugging her.

Sarah pulled away from the hug.

"You should come over for dinner tonight," Sarah said, changing the subject.

"What?" Charlie asked surprised.

"Yeah! My dad would love to see you and hear about your military stories," she said.

"I don't know," he said.

"Please! I know it will make his day," she begged.

"What are you making for dinner?" Charlie asked jokingly.

"I'll make your favorite, spaghetti and meatballs," Sarah said. "That is still your favorite, right?"

"Absolutely. I'll be there," he said with a smile.

"Alright, cool. I have to get back to work, but I'll see you tonight," she said.

Sarah kissed Charlie on the forehead and walked back downstairs to continue working. I can't believe Charlie is back in town, she thought to herself. She began to wonder what she should wear for dinner and if she still had that old perfume he liked. She couldn't wait to see the look on her dad's face when Charlie walked through the door. "You need to marry that boy," he would often tell her.

That evening, Sarah was in the kitchen preparing dinner when the doorbell rang.

"Were you expecting anyone?" Edward called to her from the living room.

"I don't know. Can you answer it? My hands are tied up right now," Sarah answered.

Edward got off of the couch and walked over to the door.

"Well I'll be damned," Edward said as he opened the door. "If it isn't Charlie sonofabitch Canton!"

"It's good to see you, Eddie," Charlie said, shaking his hand.

"Come on inside. What have you been up to? I want to hear all about it," Edward said, leading him inside the house.

The two walked into the kitchen.

"Hey Sarah, look who I found," Edward said.

"Actually, I ran into Sarah at the bookstore today and she invited me over for dinner," Charlie said, smiling at Sarah.

"I should have known you weren't here to see this old man," Edward said, nudging Charlie in the side. "Come on, have a seat. Can I get you a beer?"

"Sure. Whatever you have is fine," Charlie replied, taking a seat at the table.

"Dinner will be ready in just a few minutes, boys," Sarah said.

Edward grabbed two beers out of the refrigerator and joined Charlie at the table.

"Are you on leave right now?" Edward asked Charlie, handing him one of the beers.

"Actually, I just finished up my eight years and I got the hell out of there," Charlie said while smiling.

"And you came back to this shithole?" Edward asked laughing.

"Well, I thought there might be something here for me," Charlie said, looking over at Sarah.

Sarah blushed.

"Alright boys, dinner is ready. Come help yourselves. The plates are over here and you can make your way down the line," she said.

The three of them fixed their plates and sat down at the table to eat. Edward asked Charlie about his time in the service and the two of them shared military stories back and forth. Edward's stories mainly focused on boot camp. He didn't get into his time spent at war. They laughed a lot. Sarah sat back and enjoyed watching her dad have a good time. It was also nice to have Charlie home, she thought to herself.

After everyone was done eating, Edward and Charlie made their way into the living room to watch some TV. They both grabbed another beer out of the fridge on their way. Sarah wondered if her dad should be drinking with his condition, but she wasn't going to ruin his fun. Sarah began to clean up the mess in the kitchen and wash the dishes. Then the doorbell rang.

"I'll get it," Charlie said.

Charlie walked to the front door and opened it. It was Tim.

"Can I help you?" Charlie asked.

"Uh, hi," Tim said startled. He looked Charlie up and down. "I was wondering if Sarah was home."

Charlie stiffened his stance in the doorway.

"Who's asking?" he asked.

"Tim," Tim replied.

"One second, Tim," Charlie said, giving him a smirk.

Charlie turned his head towards the kitchen and yelled, "Sarah, there's some guy named Tim here looking for you. Do you want me to tell him you're indisposed?"

Charlie looked back at Tim with a smile on his face. Tim responded with a half-smile. Sarah came running to the front door, hands still wet and soapy from the dishes.

"Uh, no. That's OK, Charlie. I'll handle it. Thanks," she said, giving Charlie a look.

"Alright," Charlie said, taking his cue. "If you need me, I'll be over here with Eddie."

Charlie walked into the living room and joined Edward on the couch. Sarah stepped out onto the porch with Tim and closed the door behind her.

"What are you doing here?" she asked surprised, wiping her wet hands on her pants.

"I, uh, thought you would be getting home from work around now and I wanted to surprise you and see if you wanted to go for a walk. But maybe I should have called first," Tim said, looking towards the living room window.

Sarah followed his gaze.

"Oh," Sarah said. "That's my friend Charlie. He..."

"You don't owe me any explanation," Tim said, interrupting her. "We've only been on two dates and we never said we were exclusive or anything."

"It's not like that," Sarah said. "Charlie and I have known each other forever. He's my best friend."

"Oh," Tim said, not sure how he felt about that. "I wanted to see you since it's been a few days."

"Yeah. Where have you been?" Sarah asked curiously.

"I've been filling in at a different center the past two days," he said. "I'm sorry I haven't messaged you."

"I thought you were ghosting me," she said, pushing him playfully.

"I would never," Tim said laughing. "But hey, you didn't text me either."

"I've been busy," Sarah said, mocking Tim.

They both laughed then stood there in silence for a few moments. Sarah didn't want to invite Tim in because she could already sense the tension between him and Charlie. Plus, Charlie and her dad were bonding and she didn't want to ruin that.

"Can I take a raincheck on that walk?" Sarah finally asked.

"Sure," Tim said, sounding a little defeated.

"OK. I'll talk to you later," Sarah said while taking a step back towards the door and waving at Tim.

"Later," Tim said, returning the wave.

Sarah went inside and closed the door.

"So that's the male nurse?" Charlie asked mockingly.

Sarah opened her mouth as if to say, "How did you know?" But Charlie interrupted her.

"Your dad's been filling me in on lover boy while you were out there," he said, giving her a wink.

Sarah looked over at her dad who gave her a shrug.

"Is that so?" Sarah asked.

She walked into the living room and took a seat in the chair next to the couch.

"Why didn't you invite him in?" Charlie asked, looking at Sarah seriously.

"You afraid I was going to scare him off?" he asked, leaning forward and giving Sarah a playful nudge.

"Yup. That was definitely it," Sarah said laughing.

"Well, I'm going to go hit the hay. I'll see you in the morning, sweetheart. And Charlie, don't be a stranger," Edward said, getting off the couch.

"I won't, sir," Charlie said.

"Goodnight, dad," Sarah said.

Edward walked up the stairs and went to bed. Sarah went and sat next to Charlie on the couch. Charlie put his arm around Sarah and pulled her close to him.

"I missed you, Sare-Bear," he said.

"I missed you too, Cha-Cha," Sarah said laughing.

That's what she used to call Charlie when they were really little before she could pronounce Charlie. The two of them sat in silence for a little while, just enjoying the familiarity of each other's presence. Then Charlie pulled his arm away and sat up on the couch. He looked at Sarah with a smirk.

"Do you still have Monopoly?" he asked.

"Uh, duh," she said. "Remember when we would stay up until four in the morning playing?"

"Let's do it!" Charlie said excitedly.

"Charlie," Sarah said laughing.

"C'mon. For old time's sake," he said.

"I physically cannot stay up that late anymore and I have to take my dad to his appointment tomorrow," Sarah said.

"I'll take him. I'm used to only getting a few hours of sleep," Charlie said, not giving up.

Sarah looked at Charlie.

"Alright, fine. But no throwing the board when you lose. My dad is sleeping so we have to keep it down," she said.

"Scout's honor," he said, holding up three fingers.

Sarah turned the TV off and the two of them went up to her room.

"It's been a while since I've been up here," Charlie said, looking at all of the photos on her wall.

He found a photo of the two of them at prom.

"This was the best day ever," he said.

Sarah joined him to see what memory he was talking about.

"It was a good day," she said in agreement.

Charlie turned around and went to her game collection. He pulled out Monopoly and turned around with the biggest grin on his face.

"You ready to get your ass kicked?" he asked.

"Bring it on," Sarah replied.

The two of them sat down on the bedroom floor and set up the game. They took turns rolling the dice and buying properties until there were only two left – Park Place and Marvin Gardens. Charlie needed Park

Place for a monopoly and Sarah needed Marvin Gardens. The other colors were evenly divided with neither of them having a monopoly. It was Charlie's turn. He rolled a four, which put him on Park Place.

"Yes!" he quietly shouted.

"You're mine now," he said, turning towards Sarah.

Sarah was sound asleep on the floor. Charlie let out a laugh. He moved the game aside and picked Sarah up off the floor. He carried her over to her bed and covered her up with the comforter. He gave her a soft kiss on the forehead and whispered "sweet dreams." Then he put Monopoly away.

He looked at her bed and wondered if he should climb in there with Sarah or go sleep on the couch. The two of them have shared a bed several times in the past, but it had been a while. He didn't know if Sarah would still be comfortable sleeping with him. So as much as he wanted to cuddle up to his best friend, he grabbed a blanket and went and slept on the couch.

5

The next morning, Charlie was the first one awake. He went into the kitchen, started a pot of coffee and began cooking breakfast. Edward wandered into the kitchen shortly after.

"Well isn't this a pleasant view," Edward said.

Charlie turned around and gave Edward a smile.

"Morning, Eddie! I hope you don't mind that I crashed on the couch last night," Charlie said.

"Not at all. You know you're welcome here any time," Edward said, making his way to the table to sit down.

"Coffee?" Charlie asked, holding up the freshly brewed pot.

"Sure," Edward responded.

Charlie poured Edward a cup of coffee and took it to him at the table.

"I told Sarah I would take you to your appointment this morning so she could sleep in," Charlie said.

"Oh, good," Edward said. "That girl works too hard and is always on the go. She needs some rest."

Edward and Charlie ate their breakfast and then went to Edward's radiation appointment. Sarah woke up shortly after they left. She made her way downstairs and found a note next to the coffee pot. It read, *Sare-Bear, the coffee is hot and there are some pancakes in the fridge. Have a good day at work. Love, Charlie.* Sarah smiled and poured herself a cup of coffee. It was nice having Charlie home, she thought to herself.

Later that day, Sarah went to work her shift at the bookstore. It was a slow day compared to the day before. Wednesdays usually were. She was organizing the books in the back room. She was about four hours into her shift when Cindy walked in with that annoying smile on her face.

"I wish I had your life," Cindy said with a sigh.

"What are you talking about?" Sarah asked confused.

"There's another guy here asking for you," Cindy said.

"What?" Sarah asked.

"Yeah, he's in the front of the store," Cindy replied.

Sarah walked into the front of the store and saw Tim standing there with a brown paper bag and a bouquet of wildflowers.

"Hi," he said with a smile on his face. "Are you hungry? I brought you some lunch."

"Hang on just one moment," Sarah said with a smile.

She went back into the back room and told Cindy she was going to take her lunch break. Sarah went back to where Tim was.

"Here, these are for you," he said, handing her the flowers.

"They are beautiful," she said, taking the flowers and leading Tim to a table where they sat down.

"This is a nice surprise," Sarah said.

"I don't know what kind of food you like, so I guessed. I got you an Italian sandwich with chips from this great deli I know," Tim said. "I hope that's OK."

"That's perfect," Sarah replied.

Tim pulled a sandwich and a bag of chips out of the bag and slid them across the table to her. He pulled his sandwich out as well. The two of them ate in silence for a moment.

"I want to apologize for yesterday," Tim said.

"What do you mean?" Sarah asked, thinking back to what he could possibly be apologizing for.

"I shouldn't have showed up to your house like that. In the future, I will be more mindful," he said.

Sarah laughed. Tim looked at her confused.

"It's OK, Tim. We're cool. You don't need to apologize," she said.

"OK. I just wanted to make sure. I thought maybe you didn't want to see me and that was why you didn't take Edward to his appointment this morning," Tim said.

"What? No," Sarah said.

"Charlie and I were…," she trailed off. She didn't want Tim to be jealous of Charlie so she figured she shouldn't tell him about their sleepover. "Charlie volunteered to take my dad to his appointment. That's all."

"Well, if that's all," Tim said, grabbing Sarah's hand.

Sarah gave him a smile. Tim released her hand and the two of them continued eating their lunch.

"So, tell me about Charlie," Tim said nonchalantly.

"What do you want to know?" Sarah asked.

"Have you two ever dated?" Tim asked curiously.

Sarah put her sandwich down and looked at Tim.

"No. I told you, he's my best friend. We've literally been friends forever," she said.

"OK. I just wanted to know if I was up against anyone," he said, giving Sarah a wink.

Sarah smiled.

"Maybe you are, but it's not Charlie," she said, winking back.

"Good to know. I guess I'll just have to step up my game," Tim said. "How long of a plane ride is it to Thailand?"

Sarah laughed.

"If you take me to Thailand, that's game over for everyone else," she said.

"I'll get planning then," he said.

Tim smiled at her and took another bite of his sandwich. The two of them finished eating and sat at the table talking for a few more minutes. Neither of them wanted that moment to end, but Sarah knew she had to get back to work. She thanked him for the surprise and walked him outside.

"Thanks again," she said, smelling the flowers.

"Any time," he said. "Say, what are you doing on Saturday?"

"My dad and I have plans to go stroll around the farmer's market. It's kind of a tradition we have at the beginning of every season," Sarah said.

"OK. What about Sunday?" Tim asked.

"I think I could make Sunday work. What did you have in mind?" she asked.

"It's a surprise. I'll pick you up at 2 p.m.," he said.

"I'll see you then," Sarah said.

Tim leaned down and gave Sarah a light kiss on the lips.

"I was right. I prefer the store better at night," he said, giving Sarah a wink before walking away.

And just like that, Sarah became flushed with emotion remembering the moment they shared on the couch upstairs a few days prior. Sarah wanted Tim, all of him. She wanted to know how he felt. She went back into the store and smiled up at the stairs.

"Are you OK?" Cindy asked her.

"I'm perfect," Sarah replied. "I'm going to go finish organizing those books back there."

Sarah went back into the back room and leaned up against one of the bookshelves. I can't believe I need to wait until Sunday to kiss him again like that, she thought to herself. Suddenly, she was thirsty for Tim. He was all she thought about the rest of the day. She laid in bed that night replaying their two makeout sessions.

6

Saturday morning rolled around and Sarah was in the kitchen making breakfast for her and her dad when the doorbell rang. She wasn't expecting anybody so she looked over at her dad who shrugged. She went and answered the door and there was Charlie, looking as handsome as ever in khaki shorts and a green polo. It really brought out the color of his eyes, she thought to herself.

"Charlie! What are you doing here?" she asked while leaning in to give him a hug.

"Your dad invited me to go to the market with you guys today. You know, like old times," Charlie said smiling.

Charlie did tag along with Edward and Sarah when they were younger, but that was before Sarah really appreciated the time with her father. Her and Charlie mainly ran around and played hide-and-seek while Edward picked out seasonal décor for the house. It was something Sarah's mother liked to do before she died. After she passed, Edward kept up the tradition.

But now, with her dad being ill, Sarah was looking forward to spending this tradition with just him.

"Or I don't have to," Charlie said, examining Sarah's face.

Sarah quickly forced a smile.

"Nonsense. Come on in," she said, stepping aside to let him in.

The three of them drove to the market together, which wasn't that busy. The third Saturday in June was usually quiet as people escaped the city to go to their cottages up north. Sarah was examining her dad as he gazed at the different booths. It was almost as if he had a look of pain in his eyes, she thought. Sarah wondered if her dad was physically in pain from the cancer or if it was the memory of coming here with her mother. He never did remarry after her mother died. It had been 20-some years and he always stayed true to his wife.

"Where would you like to go first, dad?" Sarah asked.

"Let's make our way down this aisle and we'll loop around and look at the flowers last," Edward replied.

"Sweet. I see some churros up here. Who wants one? I'm buying," Charlie said with a smile.

Sarah and Edward both let out a laugh.

"Sure," they said in unison.

They continued strolling through the different booths when Sarah realized Charlie had fallen behind. She turned around to see he was a few booths back.

"You two keep going. I'll catch up," he called to her.

She gave him a thumbs up and was happy to have a minute alone with her dad. She linked her arm through Edward's.

"I'm happy we have this tradition," she said.

"Me too," he said, looking down to her.

They continued strolling until Edward stopped at a booth that sold paintings. He began flipping through the canvases when he stopped and pulled one out of the box. He held it up to show Sarah.

"Isn't this where you were?" he asked.

Sarah turned and looked at the painting.

"Yeah, that's Cinque Terre," she said.

"Do you want it?" he asked.

Sarah examined the painting closely and realized she will always associate that place with her dad's cancer.

"No, that's OK," she said with a slight smile.

Edward put the painting back and kept flipping through the rest of the canvases. He pulled out two paintings, one of a mountain and one of a coastline.

"Which one do you think would look better in the living room?" Edward asked.

Sarah looked at both paintings. The coastline painting had more colors and she associated it with being happy. But she was more drawn to the mountain painting. It was a little darker, a little mysterious, she thought.

"I like the mountain," she said.

"OK, mountain it is," Edward replied.

By the time Edward had purchased the painting, Charlie had caught up with them. He was holding a small bag.

"What did you get?" Sarah asked him.

"Oh, nothing. Just some spices," Charlie said, hiding the bag behind his back.

Sarah looked at him quizzically, but decided to drop it.

"Are you two hungry for lunch? There are some good food trucks up here," Edward said.

"I can always eat," Charlie replied.

"Same," Sarah said with a smile.

They all picked a different food truck. Sarah got tacos, Charlie got barbecue, and Edward got a chili dog and fries. They sat at a picnic table and ate their food, talking about the different booths that had come and gone over the years. Sarah looked at her dad and could tell he was tired.

"When we're done eating, I say we go look at the flowers and then head home. I could use a nap," Sarah lied.

She wasn't tired at all, but she knew her dad was and he would never say it. Edward gave her a smile.

"Whatever you want, kiddo," he said.

"That works for me," Charlie said.

The three of them finished eating and walked over to the flower booth. There were bright, yellow sunflowers, an assortment of peonies and lilies, roses, and calla lilies. Calla lilies were Sarah's mom's favorite. That's what her wedding bouquet was made of. Edward bought a bouquet of calla lilies.

"Those look nice, dad," Sarah said, putting her hand on his shoulder.

He gave her a smile. They were about to head to the car when they realized Charlie was no longer with them. Then Charlie walked out of the flower booth with a single lily in his hand.

"For you, my lady," he said as he placed it behind Sarah's ear.

"Thank you," Sarah said, giving Charlie a hug.

When they arrived back at the Simmons' house, Charlie helped Edward hang their new painting in the living room. Sarah took the calla lilies to the kitchen where she placed them in a vase in the window by the sink. By the time she made it back into the living room, the painting was already hung.

"That was fast," she said.

"Well, you have two guys who know what they're doing," Charlie said with a grin.

Edward laughed.

"I'm going to go rest my eyes upstairs," Edward said as he walked upstairs.

That's what he called taking a nap. He never said he was taking a nap. He always said he was "just resting his eyes."

Sarah and Charlie sat down on the couch.

"So now what would you like to do, Sare-bear?" Charlie asked.

He removed the flower from behind her ear and placed it on the coffee table.

"It doesn't matter to me," Sarah replied.

"We can do anything. I'll go anywhere with you," he said seriously.

Sarah looked Charlie in the eyes and tried not to read further into what he just said.

"Do you want to go for a walk?" she asked.

"Sure," he replied.

The two of them walked outside and began walking down the street. Charlie grabbed Sarah's hand and she gave him a smile. She knew Charlie liked her and she liked him. She always had. She was comfortable with him. To her, Charlie was like home. They didn't have any secrets from each other and they shared a lot of the same interests.

But now there was Tim. Sarah liked Tim too, but things were still really new with Tim. Maybe they would work out, maybe they wouldn't. She didn't know, but she knew she wanted to give them a try. So for now, she thought to herself, she would keep her feelings for Charlie at bay.

"So tell me about this Tim guy," Charlie said.

"What?" Sarah asked startled.

Was I thinking out loud, she thought to herself.

"You know, the nurse who showed up to your house the other day," Charlie said.

"Oh," Sarah said, realizing her thoughts were safe in her head. "What do you want to know?"

"Are you two serious?" Charlie asked.

"I mean, not really. We've really only had like three dates," she said.

"So have you two," Charlie said while making a circle with his left hand and poking his right index finger through it to indicate having sex.

"Charlie!" Sarah said, pushing him away.

"What? I'm curious," he said laughing.

"No, we haven't done that," she said blushing.

"Well, what have you done?" Charlie asked.

Charlie stopped in front of Sarah and grabbed both of her hands.

"We've only kissed," Sarah said, looking up at Charlie.

"Like this?" Charlie asked before leaning down and giving Sarah a light kiss on the lips.

Sarah's heart fluttered.

"No," she said. "Like this."

Sarah put her right hand behind Charlie's neck and stood on her tiptoes. She moved her head up towards his. Their lips met and she forced his lips apart with her tongue. She pushed her tongue in his mouth while pulling his head closer to her. He pushed his tongue into her mouth and picked her up off the sidewalk. Sarah wrapped her legs around Charlie's waist. Then she pulled her head back.

"Like that," she said with a smile.

"I see," Charlie said smiling.

He put Sarah back on the ground.

"Do you want to go somewhere?" he asked.

"Like where?" she asked.

"Like back to my place," he said with a childish grin.

Sarah let out a laugh.

"Charlie," she said, pushing him away.

"It was worth a try," he said with a grin.

Charlie grabbed her hand again and they continued walking.

"Where are you living now? Are you with your parents or did you get your own place?" Sarah asked. "I guess I never asked you when you came back home."

"No, I have my own apartment," he said. "You should come see it sometime."

"Yeah, I'll have to," she said. "Just not right now."

She gave Charlie a wink and pulled his hand to lead him over to the park down the road from her house. She sat down on a swing and Charlie stood behind her. He squatted down and hugged her from behind.

"I really missed you, Sare-bear," he whispered in her ear.

"I missed you too," Sarah said, turning her head to look at him.

Charlie leaned down and kissed her on the lips again. They held their lips together for a few seconds before Sarah pulled away. Charlie gave her a slight smile and stood back up. He grabbed the seat of the swing and pulled it back before releasing it. He pushed her on the swing lightly like that for a little while.

"Do you want an underdog like old times?" he asked.

"Oh no. That would be too scary now," Sarah said laughing.

Charlie laughed. Then he went and sat on the swing next to her. He didn't swing, he just sat there and looked at Sarah.

"What?" she asked.

"Nothing. I just like looking at you," he replied.

Sarah blushed and changed the subject.

"So now that you're out of the service, what are you going to do next?" she asked.

"Well, I have a lot of money saved up since you don't really get a chance to spend it in the military. So I figured I would take a few months off. Maybe do some traveling. And then either start college in the fall or enter the workforce. I'm not really sure, but I have some time to figure it out," he said.

"College is overrated," Sarah said with a smile.

Sarah never went to college. Edward offered to pay her tuition, but she graduated shortly after he was forced to retire. Sarah didn't want to be a financial burden on her dad. Besides, she was more interested in seeing the world. Plus, she didn't have a strong desire for any particular major. She didn't like the idea of being a career woman. She liked flexibility and not being tied down to one job.

"You're probably right," Charlie said.

"I usually am," Sarah said laughing. "Are you ready to head back?"

"I'm never ready to leave you," Charlie said with his gaze fixed on Sarah.

Sarah looked at Charlie and gave him a half smile. He grabbed her hand.

"Sarah, I want you to know something," he said hesitantly.

"What is it?" she asked.

"The reason I came back to Muncie is you. It's always been you," he said.

"Charl," Sarah started, but Charlie cut her off.

"No, please, let me finish. You do whatever you need to do to figure things out with Tim. But when you're done, I'll be here. I'll always be here for you," he said.

Charlie lifted Sarah's hand to his lips and kissed it. She scooted her swing over to Charlie's and gave him a hug. She rested her head on his shoulder for a little while before pulling away.

"I don't want to lose your friendship," she said.

"You won't," he replied. "I promise."

Charlie held out his pinky finger to make a pinky promise and Sarah locked her pinky finger with his. They both looked at each other with a half-smile.

"Alright, let's get you home," Charlie said.

Sarah and Charlie walked back to her house. They didn't hold hands and they didn't say anything the whole way back. When they got to the house, they both stopped on the front porch.

"I'm going to head out, but before I do, I got you something," Charlie said, pulling the small bag out of his back pocket.

He pulled a beaded bracelet out of the bag and grabbed Sarah's hand to place it on her wrist.

"Charlie," she said, almost in tears.

The bracelet was identical to the one she used to wear in high school. It was her mother's bracelet and had her and her mother's birthstones in it. Sarah lost the bracelet when they went to the beach for senior skip day. She and Charlie searched the beach and the water for hours that day, but they couldn't find it. Sarah was heartbroken. She eventually forgot about the bracelet, until now.

"When I saw it at the market, I knew I had to get it for you," he said.

Sarah threw her arms around Charlie and hugged him just as tight as she did when he left for boot camp. In that moment, she forgot about Tim. It was just her and Charlie. Charlie knew her better than anyone. He knew all of her secrets, all of her pain, the good and the bad. He was there through it all.

Sarah pulled back from the hug and looked into Charlie's dark green eyes. She leaned in and kissed him on the lips. He went to pull away, but Sarah put her hand behind his neck and pulled him closer. She slid her tongue into his mouth and wrapped her other arm around his back. Charlie, never wanting anything more in his life, kissed her back.

He pushed her back against the front door and pushed his tongue into her mouth. He had one hand on the door for support and he started sliding his other hand under her shirt, up her side. He moved his lips to her neck where he began leaving a trail of kisses up to her ear. He brushed his lips against her ear lightly.

"I want you," he whispered.

Sarah pulled back and looked at Charlie seriously.

"I want you too," she said.

They both stared at each other in silence for a moment debating if they were really going to take this next step. They both knew there was no turning back once they did.

"My place?" Charlie asked.

Sarah nodded.

7

The drive to Charlie's apartment was a blur. They both had just one thing on their mind and they couldn't wait to get there. Once they arrived, Sarah and Charlie raced up the stairs to his door holding hands. Charlie unlocked the door and led Sarah inside. He closed the door and turned around to lock it.

He turned back around and stared at Sarah for a moment. Her brown hair cascaded down the front of her shoulders. He slowly moved towards her and placed his hands on her hips. She put her hands on his shoulders and could feel his muscles through his shirt. She leaned in to kiss him. They kissed softly at first and then more aggressively. They were thirsty for each other.

Charlie pulled his lips away and lifted her shirt over her head. He threw it across the room. Sarah unbuttoned his shorts. He picked her up and she wrapped her legs around his waist. He carried her to his bedroom with his shorts slowly falling down on the way. He laid her gently on the bed and kicked his shorts off of his feet. Sarah removed her pants while he did that. Charlie stared at her laying on his bed in her black lace bra and underwear. She wasn't curvy by any means, but she had a slight hourglass shape to her.

"Wow," he said, as he removed his shirt.

"Right back atcha," she said staring at Charlie standing in front of her in just his black boxer briefs.

Sarah moved her eyes down his chest, which was perfectly chiseled with abs. Two, four, six, eight, she counted. Her eyes made their way further south on his body. She could see his bulge through his underwear. It was throbbing to get out.

Charlie climbed onto the bed on his hands and knees, kissing Sarah's body as he made his way over her. First her inner thigh, then her stomach, then her chest, then her lips. He pulled his lips away and looked her in the eyes. He slid his right hand up her left leg and grabbed her panties.

"Are you sure you want to do this?" he asked.

"Yes," she said, grabbing his face and pulling it towards her.

Sarah forced her tongue inside his mouth and moved one hand to his back while keeping the other on the back of his neck. Charlie, still holding her panties, pulled them down towards her knees. He pulled away from her lips and began kissing his way down her body. Sarah used her feet to kick her underwear off. Charlie kissed her lower stomach and then looked up at her with his chin resting on her body. Sarah looked down at him. Her heart was racing.

Charlie continued down her body. His lips were on her vagina. First, he kissed it softly. Then he grabbed one of the lips with his gently. Then he released it. He used his tongue to trace a heart around the opening. Then he thrusted his tongue inside her vagina. Sarah let out a moan and grabbed the sheet with both hands. Charlie put his hands on either side of her hips. He pushed his tongue further inside her. She moaned louder. After a few minutes, Sarah couldn't take it anymore.

"I need you now," she said in-between breaths.

Charlie kept his tongue inside of her. Sarah sat up and pulled him up towards her.

"I need you," she said, kissing him hard.

Charlie climbed over to his nightstand and pulled a condom out of the drawer. He quickly removed his underwear, revealing his penis. Sarah moved her eyes to it. It was average-size, but it had a nice girth, she mentally noted. He ripped the condom wrapper open and slid it over his penis. He climbed back over to Sarah and started to make his way over her, but she pushed him on his back and climbed on top of him. Sarah, straddling him, slowly lowered herself onto his penis, sliding it inside of her. Charlie's mouth opened and he pushed his head back into the pillow.

He grabbed each side of her hips and pulled her down until he was all the way inside of her. Sarah let out a moan and lifted her head towards the ceiling as she moved back and forth on top of him. Charlie sat up, putting one hand on the bed for support and the other on her back. He used that hand to unclasp her bra and remove it from her breasts. It dropped between their stomachs. Sarah looked down and grabbed the bra, throwing it across the room.

Charlie studied her breasts, which were rather small. Sarah was only a B-cup, but her boobs were perky. She looked at him and kissed him. He wrapped both arms around her back and pulled her down to the bed with him so they were both laying down. He rolled them over so he was on top of her, still inside of her.

He began to thrust harder while looking into her eyes. She closed her eyes and moaned louder. Sarah dug her nails into his back. That caused him to moan. He thrusted harder and faster. Sarah was practically yelling with pleasure. Then Charlie climaxed, collapsing on top of her.

Sarah wrapped both of her arms around his back and held him there. They laid there in silence for a few minutes catching their breath. Then Charlie lifted himself up on his elbows, his shrunken penis sliding out of her. He smiled at Sarah.

"That.... was incredible," he said.

"I don't think I've ever moaned that loud," she said, covering her face with her hands.

Charlie grabbed her hands.

"I loved your moans," he said.

Charlie leaned down and kissed her lightly on the lips.

"I'm going to go clean up and then I'll be back. Don't move," he said.

Charlie got up off of the bed and went into the bathroom. Sarah stretched out on the bed and smiled up at the ceiling. She heard the shower turn on. She thought about joining Charlie in the shower, but she was too exhausted to move. So she just laid there. A few minutes later, Charlie returned wearing nothing but a towel.

He walked towards the bed and dropped the towel to the floor. Sarah noticed his penis was back to its natural shrunken state. It curved ever so lightly to the left. He climbed into bed and slid under the covers. Sarah joined him and pressed her still-naked body against his side. She laid her head on his chest and could feel his heartbeat. He wrapped his arm around her and kissed the top of her head.

"Why didn't we do that sooner?" he asked.

"I have no idea," Sarah replied.

"What do you want to do now?" Charlie asked.

"Can we just lay here?" she asked.

"Of course," he replied, kissing the top of her head again.

The two laid there in silence until they both dozed off. Charlie woke up about 30 minutes later to his arm asleep from Sarah laying on it. He tried to remove it from underneath her without waking her, but she opened her eyes and smiled up at him.

"What time is it?" she asked while sitting up.

"Let me check," he said, regaining control of his arm.

Charlie checked the time on the clock on his nightstand.

"It's 7:02," he said. "Do you want to get dinner?"

"I probably don't look presentable to go out in public," Sarah said laughing.

"You look beautiful," Charlie said, leaning in and kissing her.

Sarah rolled her eyes.

"We could order takeout," she suggested.

"That works. What are you in the mood for?" he asked.

"Chinese!" Sarah exclaimed.

"I should have known," Charlie said laughing.

Charlie called the restaurant and placed their order.

"It will be here in about 30 minutes," he said.

"That gives us enough time for round two," Sarah said, pulling Charlie towards her.

"You want to go again?" he asked with a smile.

Sarah smiled and nodded. Charlie went to make his way down to her lady parts again, but Sarah stopped him.

"No, it's your turn," she said, pushing Charlie over on his back.

Sarah got on top of him and began kissing her way down his body. She stopped at his lower stomach and looked up at him. He was looking down at her. She gave him a wink and he laughed. She made her way down to his manhood and grabbed his not-quite-yet hard shaft in her hand and slowly placed her mouth over the tip of his penis. She forced it further into her mouth, sliding her tongue around it. She could feel it growing harder.

She grabbed his balls lightly with one hand and pushed her mouth down until Charlie's entire penis was inside. He let out a moan. He was fully erect now. Sarah slid her mouth up and down the shaft while her tongue danced around the sides. Charlie was breathing heavy. He grabbed her arms and pulled her up towards him.

Charlie kissed her hard before rolling her over on her back. He climbed on top of her and thrust his wet penis inside of her, raw and unprotected.

"Charlie," Sarah started to protest, but the feeling of his skin inside of her felt too good.

"Yes," she called out.

Charlie grabbed her hips and continued thrusting into Sarah.

"Harder," she called out.

Charlie pushed himself into her harder. She moaned. He moaned with her. He moved harder and faster. They were both sweating. He began to breathe heavier, until he quickly pulled his penis out of Sarah. He covered the tip with his hand to try to catch all of the cum, but some dripped onto Sarah's stomach.

"Sorry," he said with a slight smile.

He quickly got off the bed and ran into the bathroom, still holding his penis. He cleaned himself up and returned with a wet washcloth. He wiped off the residue from Sarah's stomach and made sure it didn't get on anything else. Sarah was still laying there trying to catch her breath. Charlie took the washcloth to the bathroom. When he returned to the bedroom, he went to his closet and pulled out a white button-up shirt.

"We should get dressed," he said, handing the shirt to Sarah. "The delivery driver will be here soon."

Sarah grabbed the shirt with a smile. She put it on over her head and stood up.

"How do I look?" she asked, striking a pose.

"Like someone I never want to leave my bed," he said, moving towards her.

He grabbed her tiny bare ass with both of his hands and pulled her towards him. He leaned down and kissed her with just a little bit of tongue.

"You are fucking sexy, Sarah Simmons," Charlie said, eying her up and down.

Sarah took a step back and looked at Charlie's naked body.

"You're the sexy one, Mr. Canton," she said as her eyes gazed at his abs.

Charlie gave her a smile before returning to his closet. He grabbed a pair of basketball shorts and put them on. There was a knock on the door.

"I'll get it," he said.

He went to walk out of the bedroom, but then turned around and looked at Sarah. He bit his lower lip and then gave her a smile. He turned back around and went and answered the door. Once Sarah heard the door close, she walked out of the bedroom. Charlie was at the dining room table pulling the containers out of the bag.

"I'm starving," Sarah said, taking a seat.

"We worked up quite an appetite," Charlie said, smiling at her. "What would you like to drink?"

"I'll have whatever you're having," she said.

Charlie went into the kitchen and returned with two pop cans. Sarah was already digging into the food.

"Sorry," she said slightly embarrassed. "I was really hungry."

Charlie laughed.

"Don't worry about it," he said.

They quickly ate their food and sat back in their chairs when they finished.

"I'm going to need to let that settle for a half hour before I can go again," Charlie said jokingly.

"Again?" Sarah asked with excitement.

"I mean, if you want to," Charlie said.

"Yes, please," Sarah said.

Sarah stood up and walked over to Charlie. She sat on his lap facing him with one leg on either side of him. He locked his hands together behind her lower back. She leaned down and firmly kissed him on the lips. She sat back and looked into his eyes.

"I can wear a condom next time," Charlie said looking down at the floor. "I just wanted you then and there."

"I think I'd prefer it if you didn't," Sarah said slowly.

Charlie looked at Sarah.

"Really?" he asked surprised.

"Yeah. I like how you felt," she said. "Like, I really got to feel you."

Charlie smiled at Sarah.

"But we have to be careful," she said. "I don't want a baby."

"I don't either," he said, still smiling.

"Let's go not make a baby," Charlie said, lifting Sarah up as he stood up.

"But it hasn't been a half hour yet," Sarah said playfully.

"I don't care," he said, carrying her into the bedroom.

He laid her on the bed and slid out of his basketball shorts. Sarah slowly unbuttoned the shirt she was wearing while biting her lower lip at Charlie. She would never grow tired of looking at his body, she thought. He jumped on the bed and pulled the shirt off of her. He rolled her onto her stomach and climbed on top of her. He kissed the back of her neck and slid his right hand down to her butt, grabbing it hard. Sarah began to breathe harder.

With his right hand, Charlie pushed Sarah's legs apart so he could fit between them. He slid his left hand underneath her and lifted her pelvis up off the bed. Still holding her with his left hand, he slowly pushed his penis into her vagina from behind. Sarah let out a moan. Charlie moved in and out slowly, lubricating his penis with Sarah's wetness. After a few motions, he started moving harder and faster.

Charlie sat up on his knees, pulling Sarah's hips up with him. Holding onto her hips for support, he continued to thrust into her from behind, moaning loudly. Sarah buried her face into a pillow and moaned. Charlie thrusted into her one more time before pulling out and releasing all over her back.

"I'm so sorry. I'll clean you up," he said after catching his breath. "Don't move."

Charlie ran into the bathroom and came back with a wet washcloth. He wiped all of the white liquid off of Sarah's back. Still laying down, she turned her head to look at Charlie and gave him a glare.

"We can shower if you'd like," he said with a smile.

"Yes, please," she said.

Sarah slowly lifted herself to her hands and knees and crawled backwards off the bed. She gave Charlie a playful glare and walked into the bathroom. He followed. Charlie turned the shower on and let the water heat up before they both stepped inside. They stood underneath the shower head and faced each other. Charlie leaned down and kissed Sarah. She smiled up at him. Then she turned around.

"Can you wash my back?" she asked.

"Of course," Charlie replied.

He poured his body wash into his hands and massaged it all over Sarah's back. She turned back around to let the soap rinse off. Charlie pulled her into a hug and rested his chin on the top of her head. Sarah wondered how that day was going to change their relationship. Was Charlie going to think they were in a relationship now, she thought to herself. She pulled back and smiled at him.

"I'm ready to get out," she said.

"OK," Charlie replied.

They got out of the shower and dried off. By that time, it was 9:30 p.m.

"Do you want me to drive you home or do you want to spend the night?" Charlie asked.

Sarah looked at his bed and then back at him.

"I'll stay the night," she said.

They both climbed into bed naked and Sarah nuzzled up to Charlie's side. She rested her head on his chest. He had one arm behind his head and the other loosely around Sarah.

"The other day I lied," Charlie said.

Sarah looked up at him.

"What are you talking about?" she asked confused.

"When I said our prom was the best day, I lied. Today was the best day ever," he said.

Sarah smiled at him.

"Today was a pretty good day," she agreed.

"You're amazing," he said, kissing her head.

"You're not too bad yourself," she said laughing.

That night, they didn't have any more sex. They didn't talk about their relationship or what was going to happen next. They didn't talk about anything in particular. They just cuddled, like all of their previous sleepovers. Except this time, they were naked and had experienced each other's body.

8

"I would walk you to the door, but it might be weird seeing your dad after last night," Charlie said as he pulled into Sarah's driveway.

"I don't think he'd suspect anything. And even if he did, he'd probably be ecstatic. He's been trying to get us together for years," Sarah said.

"So we're together now?" Charlie asked playfully.

"I didn't say that," Sarah said.

"I know. Just wishful thinking," Charlie said, giving Sarah a wink. "But on a serious note, I don't want things to be weird between us because of what happened last night. You know where I stand and what I want. But if you're not ready for that yet, I completely understand. We can just be friends."

"And if you want to be friends who occasionally have sex, I'm OK with that too," Charlie said smiling.

Sarah laughed and leaned over and kissed Charlie on the cheek.

"Thanks for last night and for being so wonderful," she said. "I'll see you later."

Sarah got out of Charlie's car and walked into the house.

"Late night?" Edward asked from the couch.

"Uh, yeah. I fell asleep at Charlie's watching a movie," Sarah lied.

"How are you feeling today?" she asked while walking into the living room.

"Not any better, but not any worse either," Edward responded.

"Do you need me to get you anything?" Sarah asked.

"No, I'm good," Edward replied.

"OK. I have a date with Tim in a couple hours, but I can cancel if you need me," Sarah said.

Edward looked at Sarah. He looked tired, she thought.

"You're not canceling anything on my behalf. I'm fine," he said. "How is that going anyway?"

"Good. It's good. He's a really nice guy," Sarah said.

"I like him," Edward said.

"Good," Sarah said. "I'm going to go upstairs and get ready. Just holler if you need anything."

Edward nodded his head. Sarah went upstairs and took a shower to get the smell of Charlie and his manly body wash off of her. She could not go on a date smelling like another man, she thought. It was 1 p.m. by the time she finished showering, and did her hair and make-up. She still had to get dressed, but realized she didn't know what they were doing.

I know you said it's a surprise, but can you please let me know what type of attire to wear? she texted Tim.

Casual is fine, but you might want to bring a sweatshirt, Tim texted back.

Sarah looked through her closet and decided to go with a pair of blue and white striped linen pants, a white tank top, and brown sandals. She was grabbing her Ball State University sweatshirt (even though she never went to college, she still supported her hometown school) when the doorbell rang. She looked at her phone. The time read 1:45. He's early, she thought to herself. Sarah grabbed her purse, but then heard the door close.

"I'm coming," she yelled downstairs.

Sarah rushed down the stairs to see Charlie standing there.

"Oh, hi," she said surprised.

"Hi," he said. "Eddie invited me over to throw back a couple beers. He said you have a hot date tonight."

Charlie looked hurt, she thought. How could I spend the night with him last night and then go on a date with Tim today, she thought to herself.

"Uh, yeah. Tim asked me out earlier this week. I should have mentioned it," Sarah said.

"It's fine," Charlie said, turning towards the living room.

"Do you want to go talk for a minute?" she asked.

"We're cool. Besides, it looks like your date is here," Charlie said looking out the window.

Sarah heard a car door slam. Charlie walked into the living room and sat on the couch. Edward walked into the living room from the kitchen and handed Charlie a beer before joining him on the couch. Then the doorbell rang. Sarah looked at Charlie, who had his back to her, and then at the door. She answered the door and it was Tim.

"Hi," she said.

"Hi. These are for you," Tim said, handing her a bouquet of roses.

"They're beautiful," she said, grabbing the flowers. "Come on in while I find a vase for these."

Tim walked into the house and closed the door. Sarah took the flowers into the kitchen and put them in a vase.

"So where are you taking my daughter?" she heard Edward ask.

"It's a surprise," Tim replied. "But I promise you she'll be safe."

"She better be," Charlie said.

"You must be Charlie. We didn't have the pleasure of formally meeting the other day. I'm Tim," Tim said, extending his hand to Charlie.

Charlie ignored the gesture.

"You have to disregard Charlie. He's a little protective of Sarah. He's always been like a brother to her," Edward said, eying Charlie.

Except brothers and sisters don't fuck, Sarah thought to herself. She walked back into the living room.

"You ready?" she asked Tim.

"Yup," Tim replied.

"I'll see you later, dad. Bye Charlie," Sarah said looking at Charlie.

Charlie waved goodbye without looking at her.

"Let's go," Sarah said, turning her gaze towards Tim.

They walked outside and Tim opened the passenger door of his car for Sarah. Sarah thanked him before getting in.

"I don't think Charlie likes me," Tim said after getting into the driver's side.

"It's not you. I think he's mad at me," Sarah said.

"Why would he be mad at you?" Tim asked.

"Probably because I pushed him in the mud in the second grade," she said trying to lighten the mood.

"He probably deserved it," Tim said laughing.

"So where are we going?" Sarah asked, changing the subject.

"I told you, it's a surprise," Tim said.

About 15 minutes later, they arrived at the Prairie Creek Reservoir – a park and recreation area just outside of Muncie. It has a lake used for boating and fishing, hiking trails, horseback riding trails, and campsites.

"I love this place," Sarah said with excitement. "My dad use to bring me here all the time when I was little."

"Good," Tim said smiling.

Tim grabbed a cooler out of the trunk of his car and led Sarah down to the docks where he rented a fishing boat. Sarah wasn't a big fan of fishing, but she loved boat rides.

"If you don't want to fish, we don't have to fish. We can just hang out on the boat and have a picnic," Tim said as he drove the boat away from the dock.

Sarah smiled at Tim.

"This was a nice surprise," she said.

Tim drove the boat to the middle of the lake and dropped the anchor.

"Are you hungry?" Tim asked.

"I'm starving," Sarah replied, realizing she hadn't ate anything all day.

"Well, let's change that," Tim said.

Tim laid out a blanket on the floor of the boat and sat down on it with the cooler. Sarah sat next to him on the blanket. Tim pulled out a bottle of Pinot Grigio and poured each of them a glass.

"Cheers," he said, raising his glass to Sarah's.

"Cheers," she replied.

They both took a sip of their wine.

"That's tasty," Sarah said.

"I'm glad you like it," Tim replied.

Next, Tim pulled out a charcuterie board decorated with an assortment of salamis, cheese, olives, and grapes.

"My favorite," Sarah gasped.

"Really?" Tim asked.

"Yes! I can eat meat and cheese all day," Sarah said.

"Well here," Tim said, feeding Sarah a piece of Gouda.

"Mmm," Sarah said.

"Now I'm going to feed you a grape like we're in paradise. Lean your head back," Sarah said laughing.

Sarah grabbed a cluster of grapes and held them over Tim's face. She slowly lowered it to his mouth as he used his teeth to break one off. They both started laughing. Tim smiled at Sarah. Then using his right hand, he slightly brushed a piece of her hair behind her ear. She smiled back at Tim. He leaned in and kissed her on the lips softly. He held his lips there for a second before giving her another soft kiss. He leaned back and popped another grape in his mouth, giving Sarah a wink.

The two of them took turns hand-feeding each other until they were full. They both rested their backs against the seat at the front of the boat. Tim reached over and held Sarah's hand. She turned and smiled at Tim, who returned the gesture.

"How long do we have the boat for?" Sarah asked.

Tim looked at his watch.

"About two more hours," he replied.

"I've never really been into fishing, but I can give it a try if you want," Sarah said.

"We don't have to. We can just drive around, or just sit here," Tim said, scooting closer to Sarah.

Sarah rested her head on his chest.

"I'd like that," she said.

Tim kissed the top of her head. Sarah looked up at him and he looked back at her. He lowered his head and kissed her on the lips. She kissed him back. Tim moved his left hand behind Sarah's neck and just rested it there, while still kissing her. Sarah slowly pushed her tongue into his mouth and then retracted it back into hers. Tim pulled Sarah so she was sitting on top of him. He moved his left hand so it was resting on her hip and put his right hand behind her neck.

Tim removed his lips from Sarah's and kissed the side of her neck. Then he lightly grabbed her lower earlobe with his teeth. She let out a soft moan. Tim pulled his head back and smiled at her. Sarah forced her lips onto his and slid her tongue inside his mouth again. With his right hand still behind her neck, Tim pulled Sarah's head closer as he pushed his tongue inside her mouth. Their tongues danced around each other.

Tim moved his left hand down to Sarah's butt and grabbed it firmly. She pulled her lips away from Tim's and leaned back. She gave him a smile and a light laugh.

"What?" he asked confused.

"We always do this in the wrong place. At my work, at my house with my dad downstairs, here," she said, looking around at all the other boats.

Tim sat up so he and Sara were at eye level while she stayed sitting on top of him. He rested both of his hands on her hips.

"We could go somewhere more private if you'd like," Tim said suggestively.

Sarah pictured the two of them going back to Tim's place. She wondered what he would feel like inside of her. Then she thought about Charlie and how he felt the night before. She didn't want to share a bed with another man so soon, she decided.

"Or we could take a raincheck on that idea and enjoy this boat you rented," she said, laying her head down on Tim's shoulder.

Tim kissed the top of her head.

"We can do that," he said. "But just so you know, that's two rainchecks you owe me now."

Sarah let out a laugh.

"I'm good for them. I promise," she said.

The two of them spent the rest of the time driving the boat around. They shared lots of laughs. There were a few more kisses given, but no more makeout sessions. They drove the boat back to the dock and checked it in. Then Tim drove Sarah home. Charlie's car was still in the driveway.

"Do you want me to walk you to the door or say my goodbyes here?" Tim asked, gesturing to Charlie's car.

"You don't have to worry about Charlie," Sarah said. "But we can just say goodbye here. I had a great time today. Thank you so much for everything. It was perfect."

"He stopped breathing. I did everything I could. I performed CPR until the first responders came, but I don't know if it was enough. They took him to the hospital, but they wouldn't let me see him since I'm not family," Charlie said. "I tried calling you so you could get there, but you didn't answer. I didn't know what else to do, so I came back here and waited for you."

"What hospital?" Sarah asked, processing the information in her head.

"General Hospital," Charlie replied.

"Can you take me there?" Sarah asked.

"Of course," Charlie said.

Charlie drove Sarah to the hospital. They didn't say a word the whole way. When they got there, Sarah asked the front desk what room her father was in and they let her up to see him. Charlie waited in the waiting room. Sarah stood outside the door to Edward's room for a moment. She was scared to go in because she didn't know what kind of state her dad was going to be in. She hadn't spoken to a doctor yet to learn exactly what happened.

Sarah entered the room to find her dad laying in a hospital bed almost lifeless. He was attached to a ventilator that was doing the breathing for him. He was either asleep or unconscious, Sarah thought. She broke down in tears and went and sat in the chair next to his bed. She grabbed his hand and tried talking to him.

"Dad, I don't know if you can hear me, but it's Sarah. I'm here. I'm here now. I'm sorry it took so long. I didn't know. I'm so sorry I wasn't there, dad," Sarah said crying.

There was a knock on the door. A doctor walked into the room. Sarah looked up at the doctor and wiped her tears away.

"Miss Simmons?" he asked.

"Yes," Sarah responded.

"I'm Dr. Multon. I'm the pulmonologist assigned to your dad's case. I will give you a brief synopsis of your dad's condition and then I will answer any questions you may have," Dr. Multon said.

"OK," Sarah said, looking at her dad's face.

"I want you to know myself and the entire medical team here at the hospital did everything we could to help your dad. But his cancer was too aggressive. His lungs have deteriorated and he is unable to breathe on his own. That is why he stopped breathing today," Dr. Multon said.

Sarah started crying again.

"Unfortunately, there isn't anything we can do at this point. We hooked your dad up to a ventilator, which is doing the breathing for him and placed him in a medically induced coma until you were able to get here to see him. I am so sorry," the doctor said, taking a pause to let Sarah process the information. "Do you have any questions I can answer for you?"

Sarah was silent for a moment.

"Is he going to die?" Sarah asked, already knowing the answer.

"Once we remove the ventilator, your father will be dead, yes," Dr. Multon replied, placing a hand on Sarah's shoulder.

Sarah began crying again.

"Did the radiation even help?" she asked between sobs.

In her head, she looked back at the previous weeks and saw how weak the treatments made her dad. She wondered if the treatments led to this.

"The radiation slowed down your dad's cancer. Without those treatments, this likely would have happened weeks ago. Unfortunately, the cancer was too aggressive by the time we caught it. We did everything we could and that let you have a few more weeks with your dad," Dr. Multon said.

The doctor waited for Sarah to ask more questions, but she didn't.

"You take as long as you need. When you are ready, I will be out in the hall," Dr. Multon said before leaving the room.

Sarah replayed the last few weeks in her head. She was going on dates with Tim and having sleepovers with Charlie. She should have been spending that time with her dad, she thought, but instead she was worried about her love life. She didn't know her dad's condition was that bad. She wondered if he knew. She was grateful to have spent the day with him at the farmer's market the day before. She will always cherish that day, the last day they spent together, she thought.

Sarah grabbed her dad's hands once more. She looked at his hands. They were filled with lines and dark spots from a lifetime of hard work. Edward Simmons was the strongest man Sarah had ever known. He worked 40 years at the plant building transmissions, and he would have worked longer if he wasn't forced to retire. He worked long hours and sometimes he would work seven days a week to provide for Sarah and her mom.

After Sarah's mom died, those seven day weeks became common. Sarah often thought it was to keep his mind off of her mom's death, but she later learned it was to provide her with the life she had. Sarah was grateful for how hard her dad worked to give them the life they had. She realized she never told him that before.

"Dad, I want you to know how grateful and how thankful I am for everything you did for me. You worked so hard your entire life to give me a good life, and you did. Everything I've done in my life, all of my adventures, everything, is because of your hard work. And I don't take any of it for granted. You taught me how important hard work is and how important family is. I only hope one day I can be half as good of a parent as you were. You were the best dad, and I hope you know that. I only wish it didn't have to end like this. I wish we had more time. But I know you have to go. I'm going to miss you so much, dad," Sarah said.

Sarah sat in the chair holding her dad's hands and cried. After a few minutes, she wiped her tears away. She stood up, leaned over her dad's bed and kissed him on the forehead.

"Say hi to mom for me," she said.

Sarah went out into the hallway and found Dr. Multon.

"Are you ready?" Dr. Multon asked.

Sarah nodded her head yes.

Dr. Multon and Sarah entered Edward's room. Sarah grabbed her dad's hand while the doctor turned off the ventilator. Sarah held her dad's hand as his heart slowly stopped beating and he flatlined. She held it for a few more minutes before releasing.

"Thank you for letting me say goodbye," Sarah said to the doctor.

"I'm glad we were able to," he replied.

Sarah went down to the waiting room where she found Charlie. She ran to him and threw her arms around him and started crying.

"You waited," she said.

"Of course I waited," he replied.

He wrapped his arms around her and held her tight. Sarah cried into his shoulder and neither of them said anything for a few moments.

"He's gone. Eddie's gone," Sarah said, still crying.

Charlie didn't say anything. He just held Sarah tighter. After a few minutes, Sarah pulled away and looked up at him.

"Can we go home?" she asked.

"Whatever you want," he replied.

Charlie drove Sarah home, neither of them saying anything the entire drive. Charlie walked into the house with Sarah and waited patiently as she looked around the house that now felt empty. Sarah turned to Charlie.

"Will you stay with me tonight? I don't want to be alone," she said.

"Of course," Charlie replied. "I'll grab a blanket and I'll be right here on the couch if you need me."

"Will you sleep with me?" she asked.

"Of course," he said.

The two of them went up to Sarah's room and climbed into bed. Charlie laid behind Sarah and held her close. She started crying and Charlie wiped her tears away. She rolled over to look at him.

"Thank you for being here today. For being here when it happened and doing what you could. Because of that, I was able to say goodbye. And I am so appreciative of that. And thank you for being here now," Sarah said.

"I will always be here for you, Sare-bear," Charlie said.

Charlie kissed Sarah's forehead. She gave him a slight smile and rolled back to her side. Charlie wrapped his arm around her and pulled her in close. Neither of them slept much that night.

10

Sarah and Charlie laid in bed in silence processing the night before. Sarah was making a list in her head of all of the things she had to do. She had to organize a funeral and she didn't even know where to start. She never had to do that before. She was so little when her mom died, she couldn't remember all of the planning that went into it.

"What can I do?" Charlie asked.

Sarah looked at Charlie as if he was reading her mind.

"What do you mean?" she asked.

"What can I do to help? Do you want me to call anyone? Funeral homes? Whatever you want me to do, I am here for you. Put me to work," he said.

Sarah rolled over and wrapped her arms around Charlie.

"Just hug me right now," she said.

Charlie wrapped his arms around Sarah and held her. Their hug was disrupted by the sound of the doorbell ringing. Sarah and Charlie looked at each other.

"I'll get it," Charlie said.

Charlie kissed the top of Sarah's head and got out of bed. He quickly put on his shorts - since he only wore his boxer briefs to bed – and went downstairs to answer the door. It was Tim and he was holding a bouquet of white roses. Tim looked at Charlie's bare chest.

"Is Sarah home?" Tim asked, caught off guard.

"She's still in bed," Charlie responded.

"How is she doing?" Tim asked.

"She's hanging in there, all things considering," Charlie said.

"Will you please give these to her?" Tim asked, handing the bouquet of flowers to Charlie. "And tell her I'm here if she needs anything."

"You know, it's all your fault she wasn't there. She should have been there," Charlie said with anger.

"Look, I don't know what happened. OK? I just know Edward isn't with us anymore. Can you please pass my message along to Sarah?" Tim asked.

"Yeah, I will. But if you knew her at all you would have known to bring calla lilies, not roses," Charlie said before slamming the door.

Charlie was so angry he wanted to throw the flowers away, but he didn't want to upset Sarah. Instead, he took the flowers into the kitchen and put them in a vase next to the roses from the day before and the calla lilies from the farmer's market. Then he went upstairs to Sarah's room.

"Who was it?" Sarah asked.

"It was Tim," Charlie responded.

"What did he want?" Sarah asked confused.

"Well, apparently he heard the news," Charlie said, pacing back and forth.

"Oh," Sarah said, realizing her dad was supposed to have an appointment today.

"He brought you flowers and I put them in a vase in the kitchen," Charlie said.

He stopped pacing and turned to face Sarah.

"Thank you," Sarah said, eying Charlie suspiciously.

"What?" he asked.

"Yesterday you were rude to the guy and today you're putting his flowers in a vase for me," she said.

"OK. I don't like the idea of you two together, or the idea of you with anyone else, but I'm not going to throw your flowers away," Charlie said defensively.

"Come here," Sarah said, motioning to a spot on the bed next to her.

Charlie went and sat beside her on the bed.

"I appreciate you. I appreciate our friendship, or whatever this is we're doing. I know you were upset yesterday, but I made those plans with Tim before anything happened between us. And if it makes you feel better, we didn't do anything. OK? But I have a lot going on right now. I have to figure out a lot of stuff with my dad and a funeral and all kinds of other things I don't even know how to do. I can't commit to a relationship right now. Not with you, not with Tim, not with anyone. What I really need right now is my friend Charlie to be here for me and help me through this," Sarah said.

"I am here for you. I'm not asking for a relationship. Obviously, I know that's not in the cards right now. It's just, seeing him makes me so angry. But I will try to keep those feelings to myself.

Whatever you need, I am here. I'm not going anywhere. I promise," Charlie said.

"Thank you," Sarah said. "Could you please start by calling my Aunt Susan? I don't think I can bring myself to say the words yet."

"Absolutely. I'll make the call downstairs. If you need anything else, let me know," Charlie said.

Charlie went downstairs and called Edward's sister. She was the only close relative Edward still had. Susan was the one who called Sarah with the news about Edward's cancer. She was also the one who helped take him to his treatments when Sarah couldn't.

Sarah began researching funeral homes online. She found three that she liked and made a note to call them later to discuss pricing and options. Then she realized she didn't know if her dad wanted to be cremated or buried. She wondered if her dad ever made a will with his final wishes laid out. Sarah went in the hallway and stood outside her dad's bedroom door. She put her hand on the door handle, but couldn't bring herself to go inside yet.

She went downstairs to find Charlie. He was in the kitchen making breakfast.

"I don't know if you're hungry, but you should probably eat. Also, I was hungry," Charlie said, cracking a smile.

Sarah laughed.

"I don't have much of an appetite, but I'll try to eat" she said. "How did it go with Aunt Susan?"

"She took the news better than I thought. I think she knew this was coming," Charlie said.

"Oh," Sarah said, wondering if she was the only one oblivious to her dad's condition.

"Are there any other calls you want me to make?" Charlie asked.

"I made a list of some funeral homes to check out, but I don't even know if my dad wanted to be cremated or buried. I don't know if he has a will, but I'll have to go through his things to see," she said.

"I can help you," Charlie said.

Sarah smiled at Charlie.

"I appreciate that," she said.

Charlie finished making breakfast and set the table. He made bacon, eggs and toast. Sarah only ate a piece of toast. Charlie tried to get her to eat more, but she said she wasn't hungry. Charlie ate what he could and put the leftovers in the fridge.

"We don't have to make any decisions today, right?" Sarah asked.

"We don't have to do anything you don't want to," Charlie replied.

"I just don't know what the timeline of things are," she said.

"You set your own timeline. When you're ready, we'll make calls. We'll do all of the things. And I will help you every step of the way. But when you're ready," he said.

"Can we go for a drive today?" Sarah asked.

"Wherever you want," Charlie responded.

They drove to the cemetery where Sarah's mom was buried. Edward took Sarah there a lot after her mom's death, but Sarah hadn't been in years. After a little searching, Sarah and Charlie found the gravestone. It read, *Martha (Thomas) Simmons 1950-1992*. Next to that was a line engraved that read, *Edward Simmons 1947 -*. Sarah traced her hand over that line. She stopped when she got to the dash.

"2014," she said.

"Well, this answers one of your questions," Charlie said.

Sarah looked at him confused.

"Your dad wants to be buried next to your mom," he said.

"Oh. I never thought about that," she replied.

Charlie held Sarah while they stared at the grave in silence. Then Sarah noticed a bouquet of calla lilies on the grave. She bent down and picked it up. There was a note attached. It read, *My dearest sweetheart, I'll see you soon. Love, Ed.* Sarah started crying.

"What is it?" Charlie asked.

Sarah handed him the note. He read it in silence. He crouched down and put his arm around Sarah. She cried into his shoulder.

"He knew," Sarah said. "He knew and he didn't tell me."

"He probably didn't want to worry you," Charlie said. "If anything, this says he was ready to go."

Sarah wiped her tears and looked up at Charlie.

"It must have been hard for your dad to live without your mom this long," he said.

Sarah never really thought about that. She could see the pain in her dad's eyes on some days, but she never thought her dad was sad this whole time. She didn't even know her dad still visited her mom's grave. She couldn't remember the last time she went to the cemetery with him. It had been several years. She wondered if that made her a bad daughter.

"Do you remember her?" Sarah asked, looking at the grave.

"Your mom?" Charlie asked. "Not really. We were young when it happened."

"I know. I don't really remember her either. I only remember things my dad told me," she said.

"She must have been something though for your dad to love her the way he did," Charlie said.

Sarah smiled.

"Yeah, she must have been," she said.

The two of them stayed at the gravesite for a little while before they got back into Charlie's car to head home.

"Do you mind if we stop by my apartment so I can grab some clean clothes?" Charlie asked, realizing he was still in his clothes from the day before.

"Not at all," Sarah said.

11

Charlie went into his bedroom to get clean clothes. Sarah's heart started beating a little bit faster as she recalled the events that took place there a few days prior. She wanted to go back to that day, back to that feeling, back to when her dad was still alive. She took off her shirt and left it by the door. She took a few steps towards the bedroom and removed her pants. Then she entered the bedroom wearing only her bra and underwear.

"What are you doing?" Charlie asked confused.

"I want you, Charlie," Sarah said.

"Are you sure?" Charlie asked.

"Yes," Sarah said as she moved towards Charlie.

She lifted his shirt off over his head. She kissed his chest and made her way down to his shorts. She kneeled before him and slowly unbuttoned his shorts. She pulled his shorts down and looked up at him. Charlie was looking back at her.

"You don't have to do this," Charlie said.

"Shh," Sarah said, as she pulled his underwear down.

Sarah put Charlie's soft penis inside her mouth to get it wet. She pulled it out and grasped it with her hand. She moved her hand up and down over the shaft until it started to get hard. Sarah put his penis back inside her mouth and did the same motion with her mouth. She could feel Charlie growing. She wrapped her tongue around his penis clockwise and then counter clockwise. Charlie let out a moan.

He grabbed Sarah's arms and pulled her up onto her feet. He forced his tongue into her mouth and began kissing her while pulling her underwear down to her knees. Sarah used her feet to kick them off. Charlie picked her up by the waist and she wrapped her legs around him. He pressed her back against the wall and slowly entered her with his wet penis. Sarah let out a moan. Charlie moved his lips to her neck and began kissing it.

"Harder," Sarah called out.

Charlie thrusted into her harder. Sarah had both legs wrapped around his waist and her arms around his back.

"Harder," she called out again.

Once again, Charlie thrusted into her harder. He pushed harder and harder into her. Their bodies pounded against the wall. Sarah moaned loudly. Charlie continued to push into her until he felt a release and he quickly pulled out, dripping onto the floor. He slowly placed Sarah's feet back on the ground. Her legs were trembling. Sarah went and collapsed onto Charlie's bed as he quickly cleaned up.

Charlie went and laid next to Sarah in the bed, still naked. She laid her head on his chest.

"Can we spend the day here?" she asked.

"Whatever you want," he replied. "But you should probably call your work and let them know you're not coming in."

"Oh shit! I totally forgot about work. What time is it?" she asked.

"It's a little after 1 p.m.," he said.

"Fuck! I was supposed to be there for 1:30," Sarah said.

Sarah quickly got out of bed and ran to her purse. She realized she forgot her phone at home, again.

"Can I use your phone?" she asked.

"Sure," Charlie said, handing her his phone.

Sarah called the bookstore and told them her dad had died the night before and she wasn't going to be in. They told her to take the rest of the week off and to let them know if there was anything they could do. When she hung up the phone, she began to cry. That was the first time she had said her dad "died." She told Charlie the night before, but she didn't say "died." It was something about that word that made it real, that made her realize her dad wasn't coming back.

Charlie jumped out of bed and rushed to her side. He wrapped her up into a hug and just held her as she cried. Sarah liked that about Charlie. She never had to explain herself or ask for affection, he just always knew what to do. Sahe wiped her tears away and looked up at Charlie. He leaned down and kissed her on the forehead.

Sarah grabbed his hand and led him into the bathroom. She turned the shower on and stepped inside, motioning for Charlie to join her. He entered the shower and gazed at Sarah's naked body. She grabbed Charlie's shampoo and squirted a small amount into her hand. She rubbed her hands together to form a lather. Then she reached up and began massaging it into Charlie's hair.

"Mmm. That feels nice," he said.

After he rinsed the shampoo out, Charlie did the same to Sarah. He started at her scalp and worked his way to the back of her neck and behind her ears.

"Ooh, don't stop," she said.

"I won't," Charlie said.

While still massaging her head, Charlie leaned down and kissed her shoulder. Sarah pressed the back of her naked body into Charlie. He moved his left hand down to Sarah's hip. He slowly lowered his right hand and gently caressed her right breast.

"I have to rinse," Sarah said, turning around to face Charlie.

Her and Charlie switched places so she could stand under the water. He gazed at her naked body while she rinsed the shampoo out. When all of the soap bubbles were washed away, she looked at Charlie.

"Now where were we?" she asked smiling.

"I think we were somewhere like this," Charlie said, moving behind Sarah and pressing himself against her back.

"Ah, that's right. But your hands were here," she said, moving Charlie's left hand to her hip and his right to her breast.

"I remember now," Charlie said, leaning down and kissing her neck while massaging her breast.

Sarah grinded her butt into Charlie. He lifted her right leg up and placed her foot on the side of the tub. He grabbed his now hard penis with his right hand and guided it inside of Sarah. She let out a soft moan. Charlie grabbed the curtain rod for support with his right hand and kept his left hand on Sarah's hip. He continued to thrust in and out of her as she moaned louder and louder. Her legs began to tremble but Charlie kept going. He thrusted harder and harder, until the curtain rod came tumbling down, knocking both of them down with it.

Sarah, now laying on top of Charlie in the bathtub with the shower still running, started laughing.

"Are you OK?" she asked.

"Yeah, are you?" he asked.

"I think so, yeah," she said, still laughing.

Sarah stood up and turned the water off. She grabbed Charlie's hand and helped him up. He looked at the mess and joined Sarah in the laughter.

"Well, there goes that," he said. "We didn't even get clean."

"Well, let's put this back," Sarah said, grabbing the curtain rod. "And then we can finish our shower."

Sarah and Charlie put the curtain rod back in its place and continued their shower. After they dried off, they went and rummaged through Charlie's closet for something for Sarah to wear. Charlie found an old T-shirt from high school and a pair of basketball shorts that had a string so she could tighten them.

"Now that is sexy," Charlie said laughing after Sarah put the clothes on.

"This look is all the rage," she said, striking a pose.

"If that's the case, then I better get on your level," Charlie said, throwing on a T-shirt and basketball shorts.

Sarah let out a laugh. Then she walked out of the bedroom towards the kitchen.

"Where are you going?" Charlie asked.

"I'm hungry. I'm going to raid your fridge," she replied.

"I don't think there's much in there right now," he said, following her to the kitchen.

Sarah opened the fridge. Inside, there were a few beers and pops, some condiments, eggs, and shredded cheese.

"How do you live like this?" she asked.

"I prefer to eat out," he said.

"Oh really?" Sarah asked, giving Charlie a wink.

Charlie laughed.

"You know what I mean," he said. "So what would you like? I will get anything you want."

"Anything?" Sarah asked.

"Anything within reason," he said.

"Would you hate me if I said Chinese?" she asked.

"We just had Chinese," Charlie responded.

"I know, but it's so good. And there's so many options," Sarah said.

"If you want Chinese, we can get Chinese," he said.

"Really?" Sarah asked.

"Really," Charlie replied.

Sarah grabbed the Chinese takeout menu off of the fridge and picked out what she wanted. Charlie called and placed the order.

"It will be here in about 20 minutes," he said.

"That's fast," she said.

"It's a Monday afternoon. I can't imagine they're very busy right now," Charlie said.

"Oh yeah," Sarah said, realizing it's not a weekend.

"Do you want a massage while we wait?" Charlie asked.

"That sounds wonderful," Sarah replied.

Charlie led Sarah into the bedroom where she took her shirt off. She laid on the bed on her stomach and Charlie climbed on top of her, straddling her butt. He began massaging her lower back, moving his hands in circular motions to work out all of the tension spots. Then he made his way up her back until he reached her shoulder blades. He could feel a lot of knots built up so he used his knuckles to try to work them out. Sarah winced a little.

"I'm sorry. I was trying to get these knots out," Charlie said.

"It's OK," Sarah said.

Charlie made his way to her shoulders and began to rub them. He moved the skin back and forth with his fingers. Sarah let out a soft moan. He pushed his fingers down deeper into her skin and began to massage harder. Then there was a knock at the door.

"No," Sarah whined.

Charlie let out a laugh.

"We can pick this back up after we eat," he said.

He climbed off of Sarah and went and answered the door. It was the delivery driver. Charlie tipped him and brought the food inside. He and Sarah ate their food in silence. Charlie examined Sarah as she thought about all of the things she still had to do with the funeral. Then she thought about the house and all of her dad's other assets. She didn't know anything about her dad's finances. The thought of it all overwhelmed her.

"Are you OK?" Charlie asked her after a few minutes.

"I guess. I just don't know what to do. There's so much to do. I don't even know where to begin," she said.

"We'll figure it out. I'll help you every step of the way. Any task that you don't want to do, just throw it at me and I'll get it done," he said.

Sarah smiled at Charlie.

"Thank you," she said.

"No problem," Charlie replied.

"I know I said I wanted to spend the day here, but is it OK if we go back to my house after we eat? I would like to start knocking some of these things out," Sarah said.

"Whatever you want," Charlie said.

12

Sarah stood on the front steps leading to her house for a few moments before opening the door. Once inside, she slowly walked around the first floor, not saying anything. Charlie stood by the front door and watched her.

"You can take your bag up to my room, if you'd like," Sarah said, making her way back towards the front door.

"OK," Charlie said.

He kissed Sarah on the forehead and went upstairs. Sarah slowly walked into the office, her dad's office, and looked around. She flicked the light on and made her way over to Edward's desk. There were papers piled on top of it. She picked a piece of paper up, it was a mortgage statement. The balance was $0.00.

OK, so the house is paid off, she thought to herself. She moved her eyes across the pile and saw an envelope labeled *Sarah*. She picked it up and held it in her hands. She pulled out Edward's computer chair and slowly sat down in it, looking at the envelope.

"What's that?" Charlie asked, entering the room.

"I don't know. I think my dad left me a letter," she said slowly.

"Oh. Well, I'll be out here if you need me," Charlie said before he went into the living room.

Sarah carefully turned the envelope over and opened it. There was a letter inside. She pulled it out and read it.

My dearest Sarah,

You may be angry with me for not telling you the severity of my condition, but I hope you know I had your best interest at heart and I didn't want to worry you. I accepted my time has come and I hope you will too. I know this is difficult for you, but please don't mourn me too long. I am going to a better place and I cannot wait to be reunited with your mom.

She was and always will be the love of my life, and it has been incredibly difficult for me living these past two decades without her. The only thing that kept me going was you. I see so much of your mother in you. You have her eyes, and her curly brown hair. And her sense of adventure.

Before we got married, your mom loved to travel. She went all over, even a lot of the same places you visited. There's a box of photos under my bed of her adventures. I hope you take the time to go through them and see your mother for the wonderful woman she was.

I really wish you had the chance to know her because you are so much like her. And you meant everything to her. As you know, your mom and I had a hard time getting pregnant. We tried everything for years to conceive, but nothing worked. We had just about given up when a miracle happened, you. You were our little miracle. And your mom loved you so much. Don't ever forget that.

I made all of my final arrangements ahead of time so you don't have to worry about any of that. When you're ready, call Smith's Funeral Home and tell them you're my daughter. Everything has already been paid for. Also, the house is completely paid off and I put it in your name. Sell it, live in it, whatever you want. It's yours. I don't have any outstanding bills or debt. So the money in my account is also yours. All of my banking information is in the bottom right drawer of my desk. You are listed as my beneficiary so there shouldn't be any issues.

Finally, I want you to be happy and live your life to the fullest. Whether that's with Charlie, or Tim, or some other guy – or girl – I just want you to be happy. You know I love Charlie, I always have. But Tim is a good guy too. Just be happy. I am incredibly proud of the woman you have become and I look forward to continue watching you grow as a person. Because I will always be with you darlin', no matter what. Except in the bedroom. I don't want to see that.

So to my dearest Sarah, do not weep for me for I am no longer in pain. Take care of yourself and be happy! And I hope you know how much I love you.

Love always,
Dad

Sarah wept quietly and then quickly wiped her tears away. Her dad was no longer in pain and he was reunited with her mom – or so he thought. Sarah didn't know if she believed in Heaven. She was never a religious person so she didn't put much thought into the idea. Sarah placed the letter back onto the desk and went and joined Charlie in the living room.

"Everything is done," she said.

"Really?" Charlie asked surprised.

"Yeah. I guess my dad took care of everything ahead of time. I just have to call the funeral home," she said.

"I can do that if you'd like," Charlie said.

"That's OK. Thank you though," Sarah said. "I'll call them tomorrow."

Charlie got off of the couch and went and wrapped his arms around Sarah. She hugged him back.

"I don't want to be alone," she said.

"You're not alone," Charlie replied.

"I'm not talking about right now," Sarah said, pausing. "I mean after this. After the funeral. I don't want to come home to an empty house."

Charlie pulled away from the hug and looked at Sarah.

"What are you saying?" he asked.

"I'm saying, or asking really, would you want to move in with me?" Sarah asked, looking up at Charlie.

"You want us to be roommates?" Charlie asked.

"Or something more," Sarah said, pulling Charlie close.

Charlie hugged Sarah again and kissed the top of her head.

"Let's revisit this idea in a few days. I don't want you to make any hasty decisions you will later regret," Charlie said.

"I thought you wanted to be with me," Sarah said, pulling away and feeling a little hurt.

"I do. More than anything," Charlie said, grabbing Sarah's hands. "But I don't think that's a decision we should be making right now. That's all I'm saying."

Sarah looked up at Charlie.

"OK," she said.

"In the meantime, I'm not going anywhere," he said, pulling her back in for another hug.

"Promise?" Sarah asked.

"I promise," Charlie replied. "I love you Sare-bear."

It wasn't the first time he had told her those three words. They used to say it often growing up and in high school. Then when Charlie went into the service, he ended all of his letters to Sarah with *I love you.* When Sarah responded, she usually said it back. But her responses became less and less in recent years. She didn't say it back in that moment.

She didn't know if she loved Charlie the same way he loved her, or if it was more of a friendly kind of love. One thing she knew for sure was she was grateful to have Charlie there with her to help her through this difficult time. He had always been a good friend to her. And he wasn't a bad lover either, she thought.

Sarah pulled her head back and looked at Charlie. He looked down at her. They both leaned in and kissed each other on the lips. It was a soft kiss, but they held it for a few seconds before pulling away. They smiled at each other and went back to hugging.

"I could hold you forever," Charlie said.

"I wouldn't mind that," Sarah replied.

Charlie picked Sarah up and carried her in his arms over to the couch. He sat down, holding her in his lap. She nuzzled her head into his chest. Charlie grabbed the blanket that was on the back of the couch and wrapped it around them. They both gently dozed off into a nap. They were woken up about 45 minutes later to the doorbell ringing. Sarah looked at the clock on the wall. It was about 7:45 p.m.

"I'll get it," she said.

"Are you sure?" Charlie asked.

"Yeah, I got it," Sarah said, getting off of the couch.

Sarah went and answered the door. It was Tim. He leaned in and hugged her tight. She half hugged him back.

"How are you doing?" he asked.

"Um, I'm OK," she said. "What are you doing here?"

"You haven't responded to any of my texts so I've been worried about you. I wanted to make sure you were OK and I want to be here for you," Tim responded.

"I'm sorry, Tim. I haven't looked at my phone all day," Sarah said.

"Oh, I understand," Tim said. "Do you need anything? Is there anything I can do?"

Charlie walked to the door and stood beside Sarah. He placed his arm around her waist. Sarah took a step away from Charlie and looked at him. Then she looked at Tim and back to Charlie.

"Charlie, can you give us a moment please?" she asked.

"Of course, babe," Charlie said, leaning down and kissing Sarah's head.

Charlie walked back into the living room. Sarah stepped out onto the porch with Tim and closed the door.

"'Babe?'" Tim asked, quoting Charlie.

"What are you doing here?" Sarah asked again.

"Are you seeing him?" Tim asked.

"I wouldn't say that. But some things have happened between us and I think it's only fair that you know that," Sarah said.

Tim looked hurt.

"I like you, Tim. I do. But I have a lot going on right now and I don't think this is the best time for me to be getting involved with anyone new," Sarah said.

"But it's a good time to be getting involved with him?" Tim asked, becoming angry.

"I didn't say that," Sarah replied.

"You didn't have to," Tim said.

"You don't even know Charlie," Sarah said, raising her voice.

"I know he's using this situation to manipulate you," Tim responded.

"You don't know anything, Tim. And I don't appreciate you coming here and starting shit when I'm trying to grieve my dead dad," Sarah yelled.

"You're right. I don't know anything because you're clearly not the type of person I thought you were," Tim said.

Tim stormed off to his car and drove away. Sarah went back into the house and slammed the door.

"Is everything OK?" Charlie asked.

"What the fuck is wrong with you?" Sarah yelled.

"What are you talking about?" Charlie asked confused.

"'Babe?' You were deliberately trying to start shit with Tim," Sarah said.

"You said you wanted something more," Charlie said, getting off of the couch.

"And you said we'll revisit that idea," Sarah said, still raising her voice.

Charlie walked over to Sarah.

"You're right," he said, grabbing Sarah's hands. "This is my fault. I guess I wanted to make Tim jealous or something. I don't know. I wasn't thinking. I'm sorry."

Sarah sighed heavily.

"It's probably for the best. He was kind of clingy. I mean, who shows up to someone's house twice in one day? If I wanted to see you, I would call or something," she said.

Charlie let out a light laugh.

"See? I saved you from another stage five clinger," he said.

Sarah rolled her eyes at Charlie and walked towards the kitchen. Charlie followed.

"Remember Adam McIntyre?" Charlie asked.

"Oh my God. I forgot about Adam," Sarah said laughing.

Sarah opened the freezer and pulled out a tub of ice cream.

"He would wait by your locker every morning before class. I had to tell him I got you pregnant for him to finally leave you alone," Charlie said.

"Yeah, thanks for that," Sarah said, grabbing two spoons out of a drawer. "Everyone at school really thought I was pregnant for months!"

Sarah carried the ice cream and the spoons to the kitchen table and sat down.

"Yeah, but it all worked out," Charlie said, taking a seat and grabbing a spoon.

"For you. Everyone thought you were so cool for getting laid. Meanwhile, I was the pregnant slut," Sarah said, opening the ice cream.

"I meant, it kept the rest of the guys away so I could escort you to prom," Charlie said.

Sarah glared at Charlie.

"Look how much fun we had that night. You know you wouldn't have had more fun with anyone else," he said.

"That's probably true," Sarah said, scooping a spoonful of ice cream into her mouth.

Charlie smiled at her and grabbed some ice cream with his spoon. As the two of them sat in silence and ate the frozen treat, Sarah thought back to their prom night. She wore a silver and white ball gown style dress that hung off her shoulders. Charlie had on a classic black tuxedo with a silver bowtie. She remembered thinking how handsome he looked that night. She also remembered realizing she had feelings for Charlie as they slow danced to Mariah Carey's "We Belong Together."

Whenever the chorus played, Charlie sang the lyrics in her ear. But only that part. Sarah didn't think much of it at the time, but looking back she realized he meant it. She also remembered blaring that song in her room after Charlie left for boot camp. She would sing the part about leaving at the top of her lungs. Edward would yell at her to turn the music down. He hated that song. But Sarah continued to overplay it that summer. She let out a laugh thinking about those memories.

"What?" Charlie asked, putting his spoon down.

"Oh nothing. I was just reminiscing," Sarah replied.

"About what?" Charlie asked.

Sarah smiled at Charlie and put her spoon down.

"Can I see your phone?" she asked.

"Sure," Charlie said confused.

Sarah pulled up the song on YouTube and turned the volume up on Charlie's phone. She stood up and grabbed his hand.

"Dance with me," she said.

Charlie got a huge grin on his face and stood up. He put his left hand on Sarah's waist and held her hand with his right. They slow danced around the kitchen. When the chorus came on, Charlie sang it in Sarah's ear. She smiled so big and wrapped her arms around his neck, holding him close. They swayed back and forth like that for the remainder of the song.

"I can't believe you remember that," Charlie said after the song ended.

"I listened to that song a lot after you left for boot camp," Sarah confessed.

"Really?" Charlie asked surprised.

Sarah nodded her head and grabbed the now-empty ice cream container.

"It drove my dad crazy," she said laughing, while carrying the container to the trash.

Charlie laughed and grabbed the two spoons.

"Yeah, I can't picture Eddie jamming out to Mariah Carey," he said while taking the spoons to the sink.

They were silent for a moment.

"Why didn't you ever tell me?" Charlie asked seriously, turning around to look at her.

Sarah turned to face Charlie.

"Why didn't you ever tell me?" she replied.

"To be fair, I did tell you that we belonged together," Charlie said laughing.

"That was in the words of the great Mariah Carey. That doesn't count," Sarah joked.

"Would it have changed anything?" Charlie asked.

"I don't know," Sarah responded.

Would it have changed anything, she thought to herself. If she did share her feelings with Charlie back then, maybe he wouldn't have joined the Air Force. Maybe he would have stayed in Muncie and the two of them would have dated. And then maybe something terrible would have happened between them and they would have broken up, ruining their friendship forever. All of those thoughts went through Sarah's head.

"I guess we'll never know," Charlie said, walking towards Sarah and pulling her into a hug.

Sarah wrapped her arms around Charlie and just held him. After a few moments she pulled away and looked at him.

"You know, deep down I think I always knew we would end up together," she said.

"So we are together?" Charlie asked, raising an eyebrow.

"Or whatever this is," Sarah said, motioning to the two of them.

"This," Charlie said, grabbing Sarah's hands in his. "Is Sarah and Charlie. It always has been."

He leaned down slowly and gently kissed Sarah's lips. She smiled at him.

"Now let's go to bed," Charlie said.

"OK," Sarah said.

13

Edward Simmons was born April 7, 1947. He died June 22, 2014. He was 67-years-old. His obituary would tell you he was a hard-working family man, a lucky sonofabitch (his words), and a diehard Colts fan. But those who knew Edward would describe him as a great father. And that's because everything he did in the past 26 years was for his daughter.

"Are you ready?" Charlie asked Sarah.

Sarah, who had been reading her dad's obituary, put down the Friday newspaper. She used her hands to iron out her dress. It was black, like her heart in that moment. It was the day of Edward's funeral. Sarah stood up from her bed and walked over to her mirror.

"Even in mourning, you're still beautiful," Charlie told her.

Sarah turned towards Charlie and gave him a half-smile.

"I'm ready," she said.

Charlie drove the two of them to the funeral home where they were met by Sarah's Aunt Susan. The three of them arrived an hour before the service began to have some quiet time with Edward's body before everyone else got there. Charlie and Susan made sure the guestbook and Edward's photo were properly displayed while Sarah slowly walked up to the casket. This was her first time seeing her dad's body since he died in the hospital nearly a week prior.

She kept hoping she would wake up and it all would have been a terrible dream, but she wasn't sleeping. This wasn't a dream. And now the day had come for her to lay her dad to rest and say her final goodbye. She peered over the casket and looked at her dad's face. He didn't look real, she thought to herself. He was so pale and almost looked like a wax figure. She reached down and touched his hand, it was ice cold. It immediately sent a chill up Sarah's back. She pulled her hand away. She leaned down and kissed his forehead.

"I love you, dad," she whispered.

Sarah had written a eulogy to read after the guests arrived, but she wasn't sure if she had the strength to read it. She turned around to find Charlie. He was standing at the back of the room watching her. She walked towards him and pulled the eulogy out of her purse.

"Will you read this for me?" she asked, handing him the paper.

Charlie pushed the paper back towards Sarah.

"I think this is something you should do. But if you get up there and you can't read it, I will," he said.

"Promise?" she asked.

Charlie held out his pinky finger. Sarah locked her pinky in his. Pinky promises were sacred in their friendship.

"I'm going to go see Eddie before everyone else gets here. If you need me, come get me," he said.

Sarah nodded her head and watched Charlie walk over towards her dad's body. Charlie had always been close with her dad. He was the only person who could get away with calling him Eddie. Her dad hated that name, but he didn't mind Charlie calling him it. She never knew why. But she knew she could never find a man her dad liked more than Charlie. And he told her that on a few occasions.

Even after all the trouble her and Charlie had been in over the years – stealing Edward's truck, breaking curfew, secret sleepovers – Edward never stopped liking Charlie. In a way, Charlie was almost his best friend too. The two of them often hung out without Sarah before Charlie joined the service, and even when he came home on leave. Sarah appreciated their friendship because it got her out of going fishing, and other things she didn't like to do. In a way, Charlie was like the son Edward never had.

Sarah smiled thinking about the special relationship Charlie and her dad had. She made her way up to Charlie at the casket.

"I will keep good on the promise I made you," she heard Charlie tell the body.

"What promise?" Sarah asked, appearing by Charlie's side.

"It's a secret," Charlie said.

Charlie wrapped an arm around Sarah's waist and kissed the top of her head. She leaned her head into his chest and held it there. Charlie put both of his arms around Sarah, wrapping her up into a hug.

"Sarah, sweetie," Susan said, appearing next to the casket.

Sarah pulled her head up and looked at her aunt.

"Guests are starting to arrive if you would like to greet them at the entrance," Susan said.

Sarah looked toward the front of the room and saw a short line of people entering. She looked back at her aunt and nodded her head.

"I'll come with you," Charlie said.

Charlie and Sarah walked towards the front of the room and greeted the guests as they entered. Each one grabbed Sarah's hand and said something along the lines of "I'm so sorry for your loss," "your dad was a great man," and "he will be missed." It was all a blur to Sarah. Even though she was physically present, mentally she was at the casino with her dad. They were at the craps table rooting for the shooter to roll a 10, which was the point. Edward told Sarah they were going to do a shot of tequila if the shooter made the point.

Sarah felt Charlie stiffen next to her, bringing her back to the present. Her eyes focused and she saw Tim walking towards them.

"Sarah, I'm so sorry. I'm sorry about your dad and I'm sorry for the way I behaved earlier in the week. I know this isn't the time or place for this, but just know I am here if or when you want to talk," Tim said, leaning down and hugging Sarah.

Sarah hugged him back.

"I appreciate that, and thank you for coming," she said.

Tim looked at Charlie and extended his hand. Charlie looked at Sarah, who was looking at him. Charlie looked back at Tim and shook his hand. Tim walked away and took a seat. Sarah continued greeting guests until it was time for the service to begin. She and Charlie took a seat in the front, next to her Aunt Susan.

The service began with an introduction from a minister. Sarah had never met the man before that day, and she didn't know if her dad had either. But her dad picked him for the role. Edward had planned everything about the day, including the delivery of the eulogy. Sarah's stomach was in knots thinking about it. She tried to stay focused on what the minister was saying, something about life and death, but she couldn't. She felt like she was going to throw up.

Charlie put his hand on Sarah's knee and that helped. She gave him a slight smile and he smiled back. Then her aunt took the podium and read a poem by Christina Rosetti. It was titled "Let Me Go."

After the poem, Charlie read a statement he prepared. He wouldn't let Sarah read it ahead of time so she didn't know what he was going to say, but she wasn't worried. Charlie loved her dad and he loved him. They had a special relationship, so Sarah wasn't surprised when she saw her dad picked Charlie to say something at his funeral.

"For those of you who don't know me, my name is Charlie Canton. Edward, or Eddie as I called him, often called me the son he never had. I've known Eddie most of my life, ever since I met his daughter in preschool. Sarah and I have been inseparable ever since we were 4-years-old.

So I spent a lot of time at the Simmons' household. And Eddie always made me feel welcomed, even when I was a teenage boy after his daughter's heart. Sarah may not have known it, but Eddie certainly did. He and I often had long talks, and Sarah darlin', you were the subject of most of those talks.

I always felt comfortable talking to Eddie. I could tell him things I couldn't even tell my own dad. Eddie was cool like that. He never made you feel ashamed or embarrassed about anything. He was the best dad, even though he wasn't mine. Everyone here can attest to that.

Eddie loved you Sarah with all of his heart and I hope you know that. He was and is so proud of you. I can only hope that I am half the dad he was if I ever have kids.

So everyone, if you could please raise your imaginary beer, because we all know Eddie would like us to be celebrating with a cold one. Eddie, here's to you and your legacy. I hope you're dancing with your wife and drinking a cold brewski. I love you, man," Charlie said.

Sarah wiped a tear from her eye.

"That was beautiful," she told Charlie after he sat back down.

"Thanks. Now it's your turn," he said. "You can do this."

Sarah let out a deep breath and looked at the podium. She looked back at Charlie who nodded at her in encouragement. She walked up to the podium.

"I want to thank everyone for coming out to celebrate my dad's life. For those of you who don't know me, I am Edward's daughter, Sarah. I never imagined myself delivering his eulogy, but here we are. I guess part of that is because he always seemed larger than life to me. He was a real life superhero and I never thought he could die. I mean, I knew he would eventually. Everybody has to, right? But he seemed invincible to me. There wasn't anything he couldn't do.

He was the person I turned to for all of my problems and he solved every single one of them. Except this one. Cancer was the one problem he couldn't solve. His one battle he couldn't win. But I'm not here to talk about that. I'm here to talk about his life.

My dad was a veteran, a husband, and the greatest dad. He was a hero. A superhero. At least in my eyes. He was my biggest supporter and encouraged me to go after all of my dreams, even when they took me halfway across the planet. He made it seem like there wasn't any goal I couldn't reach.

In high school, after working a 12-hour day, he would come to all of my afterschool events. There wasn't a play or tennis match that he missed. He was always there cheering me on. And if I didn't get the part I wanted, or if I had a bad match, he was always there to pick me up and encourage me to try harder next time. He never let me give up and that's the kind of person he was. He never gave up, on anything.

As most of you know, my mom passed away when I was young. She was the love of my dad's life and he never gave up on that love. Even decades later, he still loved her just as much as he did on their wedding day. He still brought her flowers and celebrated the traditions she started. Even though I have a gaping hole in my heart right now, it brings me comfort thinking he is reunited with his love.

My dad was the strongest man I had ever known. He was a hard worker and he worked his butt off to provide for his family. And he was selfless, so selfless. He never did anything for himself. And he should have, because he deserved the best. But that wasn't the type of person he was. He was always the last one to eat because he wanted to make sure there was enough for everyone else first. He would wear clothes that had holes in them, even though he had money to buy new ones. But he didn't spend money on himself, not when there were other things that money could be used for.

He often paid for strangers' tabs when we went out to eat. He didn't know them, but he always did kind things like that. If I had to describe my dad in a few words I would say he was selfless, loving, and kind. And those are characteristics I think everyone should try to have. Everyone in this room is better for having known my dad. And I just hope we all can strive to be more like him. Because he was the best," Sarah read.

Sarah went back to her seat.

"Your dad would be proud," Charlie said, grabbing her hand.

Sarah gave Charlie a half-smile and squeezed his hand. The minister went back to the podium and said a few final words. He called the pallbearers up to carry the casket out, which included Charlie.

"I'll meet you outside," he whispered in Sarah's ear before walking to the casket.

The pallbearers lifted Edward's casket and followed the minister outside where the hearse was waiting. Sarah cried as her dad's casket was carried out of the funeral home. She and her Aunt Susan followed behind, leading the rest of the guests outside. Charlie was waiting for Sarah by the door. He grabbed her hand and led her to his car, which was first in the procession line.

Charlie and Sarah didn't say anything on the way to the cemetery. She looked out the window of the car and cried at all of the people who stopped and saluted the hearse. She wiped her tears away. Her dad did not want a military funeral. He didn't want any special treatment. He always considered his time in the service a civic duty and nothing to be celebrated. But Sarah still requested he be buried with an American flag.

They arrived to the cemetery and Sarah and Charlie waited in the car as the rest of the vehicles pulled in behind them. Charlie grabbed Sarah's hand and she turned to look at him.

"You are showing incredible strength today, Sarebear. I'm so proud of you. And I know Eddie is too," Charlie said.

"Thank you for being here. I couldn't imagine doing this without you," she replied.

Charlie lifted her hand to his lips and kissed it. At that moment, the minister appeared outside the car and nodded to Charlie. It was time to begin. Charlie looked at Sarah and she nodded. They both exited the car and made their way to the hearse.

Charlie and the rest of the pallbearers lifted the casket out of the hearse and began carrying it to the plot. Sarah was then joined by her Aunt Susan and they followed behind the casket. The rest of the guests followed behind them. They stopped when they reached the burial site and formed a half circle around it.

The minister said a few words before the casket was lowered into the ground. Sarah grabbed a handful of dirt with her hand and dropped it on top of the casket. Her Aunt Susan did the same, followed by Charlie. Susan and Charlie both grabbed one of Sarah's hands and they stood there in silence for a moment.

"I'm OK," Sarah said, looking at both of them.

The three of them turned around to see the guests dispersing back to their vehicles. Sarah noticed Tim standing in the distance looking at her.

"I'll be right back," she said.

Sarah walked towards Tim as Charlie stayed back with her Aunt Susan.

"Hi," Tim said awkwardly.

"Hi," Sarah responded.

"It was a nice service," Tim said.

"Thanks. My dad planned it all," she said.

Tim looked over at Charlie and back at Sarah.

"Look, I know you have a special relationship with Charlie. And I'll probably never understand it, but that's OK. I like you, Sarah. And if there's any way I could see you again, I would really like to. I know I'm crazy and we hardly know each other, but I've never met anyone like you. And I don't want to just let that go because we got into a fight," he said.

Sarah grabbed Tim's hands.

"I'm going to need some time to grieve, but when I'm ready, maybe we can get coffee or something," she said.

"I would like that very much," Tim said.

Sarah smiled at him.

"And if you need anything, I'm here. And I mean it, anything," Tim said.

"I appreciate that," she said. "Thank you for coming."

Sarah leaned into Tim and hugged him. She pulled away after a brief moment and he gave her a smile before leaving towards his car.

"What did lover boy want?" Charlie asked, suddenly appearing behind Sarah.

"To pay his respects," Sarah said, turning around to face him.

"Yeah?" Charlie asked.

"Yeah," she said.

"That's all?" he asked.

Sarah turned back around and watched Tim get into his car. Charlie wrapped his arms around her from behind. She held his arms.

"He wants to see me," she said.

"Are you going to see him?" Charlie asked.

"I don't know," Sarah responded.

They stood there holding each other in silence for a moment before they got into Charlie's car to head home. That night, the two of them went to bed together like they had every night since Edward's passing.

"What did you promise my dad?" Sarah asked Charlie as they laid in her bed.

"What are you talking about?" he asked.

"At the funeral, I heard you tell him you would keep your promise. What promise was that?" she asked.

"I told you, it's a secret," he said, kissing her neck.

Sarah rolled over to face Charlie and looked him in his eyes.

"What?" he asked.

"You're not going to tell me?" she asked.

"It's not a big deal," Charlie responded, pushing Sarah's hair behind her ear.

"Then why won't you tell me?" Sarah persisted.

"Will you please drop it?" Charlie asked.

Sarah looked at Charlie annoyed.

"You really want to know?" he asked.

Sarah nodded her head. Charlie propped himself up on his elbow and leaned over Sarah.

"I promised him," he said, leaning down and kissing Sarah on the lips. "That I would keep the promise a secret."

Charlie smiled. Sarah flirtatiously pushed him away.

"You're a jerk," she said.

Charlie laughed.

"Maybe," he said. "But I'm your jerk."

Sarah rolled her eyes.

"Come here," he said, pulling Sarah close so he was spooning her.

The two of them fell asleep holding each other.

I

14

Monday, June 30 was Sarah's first day back to work since her dad died. She thought it was going to be weird, but it wasn't. She felt like she was slowly getting back to normal. Sarah was back on day shift since she no longer had to take her dad to his morning appointments. She was working on the computer in the back room putting together the store's order list for the month when Cindy walked in.

"One of those guys is here again. He didn't ask for you or anything, but I just thought you would want to know he's here," Cindy said.

"Which guy?" Sarah asked, looking up at Cindy.

"The short one. Well, neither of them were really short, but the shorter one," Cindy said.

Sarah walked into the main part of the store to see who Cindy was talking about. She glanced around the room and saw Tim standing near a bookshelf. He was with a woman. She was about Sarah's height and had long blonde hair, but she was turned away from Sarah so Sarah could only see her backside. Sarah walked over towards them.

"Tim?" Sarah asked.

Tim turned around and look surprised.

"Sarah! I didn't expect you to be working," he said.

"Uh, yeah. Today is my first day back," she said, looking towards the woman who she now realized was a girl.

"This is my niece, Charlotte," Tim said, introducing Sarah to the girl.

"Hi," Charlotte said, lifting her hand up to wave.

"It's nice to meet you. I'm Sarah," Sarah said, feeling relieved Tim wasn't there with another woman.

"Charlotte is staying with me for the week. So, I figured I would take her shopping to get a few books for her summer reading list," Tim said.

"Well, what are you looking for? Maybe I can help," Sarah said.

"I like romance novels and anything with a good mystery," Charlotte said.

"Me too! We recently got a few new teen romance novels in. I haven't had the chance to read them yet, but they have really good reviews. Let me show you those," Sarah said.

Sarah walked Charlotte and Tim over to the new releases section. The girls talked about books while Tim stood back and watched. Sarah looked over at Tim and caught him smiling at the two of them. She flashed him a smile back. In the end, Sarah helped Charlotte pick out three books. Two were young romance novels and one was a summer mystery read.

"Can I get these three, Uncle Tim?" Charlotte asked.

"Anything you want, sweetheart," Tim replied.

Being an only child, Sarah didn't have any nieces or nephews. She never really realized how much she wanted them until that moment. She was jealous of Tim and his relationship with Charlotte because she would never have that. At the same time, she thought it was extremely attractive how caring he was to his niece.

"Perfect. Follow me to the counter and I can get you rung up," Sarah said, smiling at Tim.

The three of them walked to the checkout counter where Sarah scanned the books. Tim handed her his credit card to pay.

"Uncle Tim, can Sarah join us for lunch?" Charlotte asked while the payment was processing.

Sarah looked up at Charlotte and then over towards Tim, who was rubbing his neck and looked uncomfortable.

"I don't know. Sarah, would you like to join us for lunch?" Tim asked, smiling at her.

Sarah smiled back. She looked at the clock. It was 12:20 p.m.

"I could take a lunch break," she said, handing his card back to him.

"Yay," Charlotte said.

"Let me tell Cindy and I will meet you two outside," Sarah said, handing the bag of books to Charlotte.

Charlotte smiled at Tim as the two of them exited the store. Sarah found Cindy and told her she was taking a lunch break. She joined Charlotte and Tim outside a few minutes later.

"So where are we going?" Sarah asked.

"Uncle Tim is taking us to this Thai restaurant he loves," Charlotte said.

"Tuppee Tong?" Sarah asked, smiling at Tim.

"Have you been there before?" Charlotte asked.

"I might have been there once," she replied with a smile.

Tim let out a laugh.

"Actually, Sarah and I had our first date there," Tim said.

"Wait, you two are dating?" Charlotte asked, looking back and forth at Sarah and Tim.

"Well," Tim said, looking at Sarah.

"Um," Sarah said.

Are we dating, she thought to herself. They went on a date just over a week ago, but then they got into a fight. They haven't been on a date since. And she had been sleeping with Charlie.

"I don't know how to answer that," Sarah said truthfully.

"Well, when was your last date?" Charlotte persisted.

"Last weekend," Tim replied, looking away.

"OK, well we can consider this a date. So there, you two are dating," Charlotte said.

Tim and Sarah both laughed. Sarah was going to argue with that logic, but she decided to let this 13-year-old girl think life was that easy.

"Perfect," Tim said, extending his hand to Sarah.

Sarah grabbed his hand and smiled at him. Tim extended his other hand to Charlotte.

"Uncle Tim! You're on a date. You can't hold my hand," she said matter-of-factly.

Sarah laughed.

"You're right. What was I thinking," he said, giving Sarah a wink.

The three of them walked the two blocks to Tuppee Tong. Sarah and Tim held hands the entire way. After being seated, Charlotte and Sarah scanned the menu before deciding what they wanted to order. Tim had the menu memorized and already knew what he was going to eat. Charlotte ordered a chicken fried rice dish, Sarah ordered pad Thai, and Tim ordered a spicy salmon entrée.

"I've never had Thai food before, but this is pretty good," Charlotte said after they received their meals.

"I'm glad you like it. Thai food is my favorite," Tim said.

"What kind of food do you like, Sarah?" Charlotte asked.

"I'll eat pretty much anything except seafood, but Chinese food is my favorite," she said.

"No way," Tim said. "Thai food is way better than Chinese food."

"I'm going to have to take Sarah's side on this one, Uncle Tim. Chinese buffets are where it's at," Charlotte said.

Sarah gave Tim a smirk. He let out a laugh.

"Well, I guess I'm outnumbered," he said.

Charlotte smiled at Sarah.

"So where are you from, Charlotte?" Sarah asked.

"Kalamazoo," she responded. "Same place as Uncle Tim, but now he's a Hoosier."

Sarah and Tim both laughed.

"Where did you learn that term?" Tim asked.

"It's what mom and dad always call you. Hoosier Tim," Charlotte said.

"Hoosier Tim," Sarah laughed. "I'm going to have to use that one."

"Um no, do not call me that," Tim said laughing.

"Whatever," Charlotte said, giving Sarah a smile.

"So what fun activities do you two have planned for the week?" Sarah asked.

"Uncle Tim said he's going to take me fishing," Charlotte said, making a face of disgust.

"What?" Tim asked. "Fishing is so much fun. And you've never been before so you don't even know if you hate it."

"Yeah, she's not going to like it," Sarah replied.

"How do you know?" Tim asked.

"We just know. It's a girl thing, Uncle Tim. You wouldn't understand," Charlotte said.

"So what do you recommend we do?" Tim asked Sarah.

"Take her to the movies and downtown. You could take her horseback riding or for a boat ride," she responded.

"You have a boat, Uncle Tim?" Charlotte asked.

"No, but I can rent one," he responded.

Charlotte looked at Sarah.

"It's fun. The lake is nice and you can pack a picnic," Sarah said.

"Will you come?" Charlotte asked.

Sarah looked at Tim.

"I don't want to interfere with your time together. You're only here for a week," she said.

"I don't mind. Besides, I'm sure Uncle Tim would love if you came," Charlotte said, smiling at Tim.

"Uh yeah," he said. "That's cool with me."

"Perfect. It's another date," Charlotte said, smiling at Sarah.

Sarah politely smiled back at Charlotte and then looked at Tim. He gave her a shrug and then smiled to himself as he continued eating. After they finished eating, the three of them walked back to the bookstore. This time, Sarah and Tim did not hold hands.

"Charlotte, do you mind waiting outside while I walk Sarah in?" Tim asked.

"No, that's cool," she said, smiling at Sarah.

"It was nice meeting you, Charlotte," Sarah said.

"You too. I'll see you later, Sarah! We're going to have so much fun this week," Charlotte said with excitement.

Sarah smiled at Charlotte and then looked at Tim.

"I'll be right back," he told Charlotte.

Sarah and Tim walked inside the bookstore.

"I'm sorry about my niece. She can be pretty persistent," Tim said.

"That's OK. She seems nice," Sarah said, looking out the window at Charlotte.

"Yeah, she's a good kid," Tim said.

There was an awkward pause. Then Sarah moved her gaze back to Tim.

"You don't have to come with us this week if you don't want to," Tim said. "But if you did want to, you wouldn't be imposing at all. It would actually be nice to have someone who can relate to Charlotte. She's going through a lot of changes right now and I don't know what she likes or what to talk to her about."

"I'm sure you'll do great," Sarah said.

Tim gave Sarah a half-smile.

"Well, I'll text you when I make the reservation and if you want to come, cool. If not, I understand," Tim said.

"OK," Sarah said.

"It was really good seeing you though, and I hope to see you later this week," Tim said.

Sarah gave Tim a smile. He leaned down and kissed Sarah on the cheek.

"Bye, Sarah," he said.

"Bye," she replied.

Tim turned around and walked out the door. Sarah watched him and Charlotte walk down the sidewalk until they were out of view. She turned around to get back to work when she saw Cindy standing uncomfortably close to her.

"Where do you find these guys?" Cindy asked.

"What do you mean?" Sarah responded.

"I mean, this town isn't that big and you have two beautiful men," Cindy replied.

Sarah let out a laugh.

"I don't have anybody," Sarah said.

"It doesn't look that way from here," Cindy said smiling.

Sarah rolled her eyes. Then she walked into the back room to finish putting together the order list. She sat down in the office chair and thought about what Cindy said. She had been on a few dates with Tim, but they definitely weren't in a relationship. And he knew that, she thought to herself.

But then there was Charlie. They haven't been on a date, technically, but they have been having sex. And they were basically living together. Plus, she had history with Charlie. They talked about being in a relationship, but he wanted to revisit the idea later. The conversation never came up again so they weren't in a relationship, she decided.

Therefore, she wouldn't be doing anything wrong if she decided to see Tim and Charlotte this week, she thought. But she knew that wasn't the case. Charlie would be hurt. She thought about hiding it from Charlie, but that didn't feel right either. She had never hidden anything from him.

Sarah thought back on her dates with Tim. She had a lot of fun on every one and she really liked Tim. They probably would still be dating if her dad hadn't died, she pondered, and that wasn't Tim's fault. Sure, she was with Tim when it happened, but neither of them could have predicted that, she thought. It was just bad timing and she owed it to herself and Tim to give them another chance, she decided.

Then Sarah thought about Charlie and how he had been there for her through everything. He had always been there her whole life. She had feelings for Charlie, and she did love him. But it was more of a friend love, she thought. She knew she didn't love him the same way he loved her. After all this time, her feelings should be stronger, she reflected. But she was comfortable with Charlie. He was home.

Sarah put her face into her hands. She didn't know what she was going to do. She didn't want to hurt Charlie or Tim because they were both great guys. Especially Charlie. He was her best friend and she didn't want to lose that. Sarah decided she didn't need to figure it out in that moment. She finished the order list and sent it off to the distributor. She finished up a few things around the shop and went home.

15

Sarah walked into the house and the smell of sautéed onions and garlic sauce wafted through the air. Charlie had surprised her with Chinese takeout for dinner. She walked into the kitchen and saw him standing there in a blue button-up shirt and khakis. He had set the table with candles and a fresh bouquet of calla lilies.

"What is all of this?" Sarah asked, looking around.

"Well, we haven't gone on an official date yet. So I would like this to be our first official date," Charlie said smiling.

"Charlie… it's beautiful," Sarah said, almost at a loss for words.

She walked towards Charlie. She stood on her tiptoes and wrapped her arms around his shoulders. Charlie leaned down and kissed her on the lips. She kissed him back. Then she placed her heels back on the floor and smiled up at him.

"I hope you're hungry," he said, smiling back at her.

"Starving," she said.

Charlie took Sarah's hand and led her to the table where he pulled out her chair for her. He sat on the other side of her. They took turns passing the containers back and forth, putting food on their plates. Once they had a little bit of each dish, they began eating.

"How was work?" Charlie asked.

Sarah put her chopsticks down and looked up at Charlie.

"Um, it was good," she said.

"Yeah?" Charlie asked, looking at her quizzically.

"Tim stopped by today," she said as she resumed eating.

Charlie put his chopsticks down.

"Man, that guy won't leave you alone. Do you want me to talk to him so he backs off?" Charlie asked.

"No, it was good. He was there buying some books for his niece," Sarah replied.

Charlie raised an eyebrow at Sarah.

"Really. She's staying with him for the week and she likes to read," Sarah said. "She seems really nice."

"And that's all?" Charlie asked, sounding annoyed.

"Well, she asked me to hang out with them this week," Sarah said, avoiding eye contact.

"Are you going to?" Charlie asked.

"Tim doesn't really know anything about teenage girls so I would be helping him out," Sarah said, picking her head up to look at Charlie.

"Mhm," Charlie said, picking up his chopsticks and continuing to eat.

"What?" Sarah asked, putting her chopsticks down again.

"You still like him," Charlie said, looking at her.

"Well, yeah. My feelings aren't just going to go away that fast," she said.

"What about us?" Charlie asked, putting his chopsticks down again.

"What about us?" Sarah asked.

"Do I not matter to you at all?" he asked with pain in his eyes.

"Of course you matter to me, Charlie. You matter a great deal to me," she said.

"So then what? You're just going to go off and date another guy and then come home and expect me to be your fucking house boy?" Charlie asked, raising his voice.

"Charlie," Sarah said, reaching across the table to grab his hand.

Charlie pulled his hand away.

"No, Sarah. This is fucked up. I don't know what more I can do to show you I fucking love you. I have literally always been there for you, always. And I can't keep fucking doing this if you don't feel the same way. It's not fair to me," he said.

"I don't want you to go anywhere," Sarah said.

"Well you can't date both of us," Charlie said.

"I never said I wanted to," she replied.

"You didn't have to," he said.

Charlie stood up and stepped away from the table.

"I lost my appetite. You can have the rest. I'm going to go for a walk," Charlie said, walking out of the kitchen towards the front door.

Sarah heard the door slam. It made her jump. She looked at the candles and flowers on the table. So much for a first date, she thought to herself. She had lost her appetite as well. She cleared the table and put the leftovers in the fridge.

Sarah's phone let out a ping. She walked over to her purse and pulled her phone out. It was a text message from Tim.

Hey! I rented the boat for Wednesday if you would like to join us. I know it would make Charlotte happy to see you again. Let me know and we can pick you up, or you can meet us at the park, the text read.

Sarah read the text message again. Then she looked towards the door where Charlie had stormed off. She put the phone back in her purse without replying. She carried her purse upstairs to her bedroom and then went into the bathroom to draw herself a bath. As the tub was filling up with water, she added some lavender-scented soap to help her relax.

She removed her clothes and sunk down into the tub until the bubbles were up to her chin. She began replaying the fight with Charlie in her head, but that only made her angry. She decided to think about her time with Tim and Charlotte earlier in the day. She was so happy and carefree, she thought. She realized Tim always made her feel that way.

Sarah was replaying her dates with Tim in her head when she heard the front door close. Charlie must be back, she thought. She heard footsteps up the stairs. Then there was a light knock on the bathroom door.

"Sarah?" Charlie asked.

"Yeah, I'm in here," she said.

"Can I come in?" he asked.

"Yes," Sarah responded.

Charlie opened the bathroom door and saw Sarah sitting in the bathtub. He walked towards the toilet and took a seat. Sarah kept her gaze on the wall, not looking at Charlie. He put his face in his hands. After a moment, he sat up and ran his hands through his hair.

"I'm sorry I raised my voice," he said, looking at Sarah.

Sarah didn't say anything or look at him.

"It's just something about him that makes me so mad. I don't know why," Charlie said.

Sarah looked at Charlie.

"OK, I do know why. It's because I want you all to myself. And that's not fair. Especially when you were already seeing him when I came home," he said. "I just get jealous when I picture you with anyone else because I know you and I are meant to be together."

"But how do you know that?" Sarah asked.

"Because of everything we've been through. Because of the way I feel about you. And I know you feel the same way even if you're not ready to admit it," Charlie said.

Sarah gave Charlie a half-smile.

"I'll let you finish your bath. I'll be in your room when you're done," he said, standing up.

"Do you want to join me?" Sarah asked.

"In the tub?" Charlie said with widened eyes.

Sarah nodded her head yes.

"Sure," Charlie said.

Charlie lifted his shirt over his head exposing his bare chest, which Sarah couldn't help but examine. She would never grow tired of looking at his body, she thought to herself. Between Charlie and Tim, Charlie had the better body, she decided. Even though she had never seen Tim's unclothed. Charlie then removed his pants and underwear and looked at Sarah.

Sarah moved her gaze up to Charlie's eyes and gave him a smile. She slid forward in the tub and Charlie stepped in behind her. He slid down into the water and stretched his legs out on either side of her. Sarah slid back and rested her back against Charlie's chest. Charlie wrapped his arms around Sarah's abdomen and held her close.

"This is nice," Charlie said.

"Mhm," Sarah said, closing her eyes.

Charlie kissed the top of Sarah's head. They sat there in silence for a few moments.

"If you knew baths were this relaxing, how come you never invited me before?" Charlie asked playfully.

"I don't take them that often," Sarah responded.

"Well, we should change that," Charlie said.

"I agree," Sarah said, turning her head to smile up at Charlie.

He looked down at her and lowered his head so his lips could touch hers. He kissed her gently, grabbing her upper lip with his lips. Then he slowly released. He went to pull his head back, but Sarah kissed him again. She turned over in the tub so she was facing Charlie. She moved one leg on either side of him so she was resting on her knees.

Charlie sat up so Sarah was sitting comfortably on him. She looked him in the eyes and moved one hand around his neck and the other around his back. She leaned forward and kissed him again, this time with tongue. She pushed her tongue into Charlie's mouth, which he welcomed with his. She began kissing him more aggressively and felt his manhood growing beneath her.

Sarah removed her hand from Charlie's back and slowly slid it down his body. She moved it between their privates and grabbed his penis. She held it up as she slowly lowered her vagina on top of it. Charlie let out a soft moan as he entered her. Sarah closed her eyes and lifted her head towards the ceiling.

Charlie wrapped his arms tightly around Sarah's waist. He leaned forward and began kissing her neck as she moved up and down on top of him. Then he moved his hands to either side of Sarah's waist and grabbed it. He began pulling her down harder and harder. Sara began to moan.

"Yes," she called out.

Charlie looked up at her and saw her eyes were still closed with her mouth slightly open. He continued to pull her waist down on top of him while gasping for breath. They both began to sweat from the heat of the water and the exercise routine they were participating in. Charlie began to moan again. He quickly pulled Sarah off of him as he released into the water.

They sat in the tub in silence, catching their breath.

"You're incredible," Charlie said after a moment.

"It's mostly you," she replied. "You ready to get out?"

"Yeah," he answered.

Sarah pulled the plug on the tub to let the water go down the drain. She and Charlie grabbed towels and dried off their wet bodies. They both put on pajamas and then realized it was only 8 p.m.

"Well, it's too early for bed. So what would you like to do?" Charlie asked.

Sarah looked around her bedroom and her eyes caught her bookshelf.

"I think I'd like to read. It's been awhile since I've had the chance to," she said, looking back at Charlie.

"OK," he said. "I'll go downstairs and watch TV. If you need anything, let me know."

He leaned down and kissed her on the lips. She smiled at him. Charlie turned around and walked out of the room. Sarah walked towards her bookshelf and picked out *A Summer Affair* by Elin Hilderbrand. Hilderbrand was one of Sarah's favorite authors and she often referred to her as the female Nicholas Sparks. Sarah could never pass up a good romance novel.

She sat down on her bed to begin to read when her phone let out a ping. She walked over to her purse and pulled her phone out. It was a text message from Cindy saying she was not going to be at work the next day. After replying, Sarah realized she never responded to Tim's message. She looked towards her bedroom door for a second before returning her focus back to her phone.

I would love to come. I'll meet you at the park, just let me know what time, Sarah texted back.

She let out a sigh. Charlie was probably going to be upset, but in that moment she didn't care. She went back to her bed and began reading her book. She fell asleep with the book in her hand.

16

Wednesday rolled around and Sarah was scheduled to meet Tim and Charlotte at the Prairie Creek Reservoir after she got out of work. She packed a bag with a change of clothes that she took to work with her. She had not yet told Charlie she was going to see Tim again. She decided to wait until she was already at work. She sent him a quick text that read, *I won't be home until later. I'm going to hang out with Tim and Charlotte. Don't be mad.*

By the time her work day ended, Charlie still had not texted back. She decided to push Charlie out of her thoughts and enjoy the day Tim had planned. She quickly changed into something more casual in the bathroom at work before heading to the park to meet Tim and Charlotte. Once she arrived to the park, she saw the two of them waiting for her in the parking lot. Charlotte got a huge smile on her face and began waving frantically when she saw Sarah. Sarah laughed to herself and waved back.

She got out of her car and walked over to meet them. Charlotte ran up to her and hugged her, catching Sarah off guard.

"I'm so happy you came," Charlotte said.

"Me too," Sarah said, hugging her back.

Sarah looked at Tim confused and he just shrugged his shoulders. Charlotte pulled away and smiled at Sarah. Tim walked over and gave Sarah a hug as well.

"I'm happy you came too," he whispered in her ear.

Sarah smiled at him as he pulled away.

"You know, it's OK if you two kiss in front of me. I'm not a little kid anymore, Uncle Tim," Charlotte said.

Tim and Sarah both let out a laugh.

"Maybe later," Tim said, giving Sarah a wink.

Sarah blushed.

"Alright, let's go," Charlotte said, leading the way down towards the dock.

Tim checked in at the booth and received the key for the boat. The three of them climbed aboard and Tim slowly maneuvered away from the docks. Charlotte went and sat at the front of the boat while Sarah stayed next to Tim. It was hard to hear over the motor of the boat and the wind as they zoomed across the lake so the three of them didn't talk much. Occasionally, Charlotte would turn around and smile at the two of them. Sarah laughed whenever she did that.

After a few minutes of driving around the lake, Tim slowed the boat down and coasted to a stop.

"This is a good place to anchor down," he said.

Tim moved to the back of the boat and dropped the anchor into the water.

"Are you two ladies hungry?" he asked.

"I'm starving," Charlotte responded.

Sarah laughed.

"Me too," she said.

Charlotte gave Sarah a smile. Tim pulled out the cooler and opened it up.

"What would everyone like to drink? We have wine, pop, juice, and water," he said.

"I'll have some wine," Charlotte said.

Sarah and Tim both looked at her.

"I'm just kidding," she said while laughing. "I'll take a pop."

"I'll have some wine," Sarah said, giving Charlotte a wink.

Tim handed out the drinks and then began passing the food out. He had made turkey sandwiches topped with lettuce, tomato and mayonnaise. He also brought vegetables and a ranch dip, and then strawberry shortcake for dessert.

"This is quite a spread you two made," Sarah said.

"It was all Uncle Tim. I just helped cut up the vegetables," Charlotte said.

Sarah looked at Tim and he just shrugged.

"Well I appreciate it. Thank you," Sarah said smiling.

"Any time," he replied.

The three of them ate their food while Charlotte shared her favorite stories about Tim with Sarah.

"And one time when Uncle Tim came to visit, I think I was about 7 or 8-years-old, he said we could play barber shop. Except he meant pretend and I thought he meant I could cut his hair. So I pulled out the kitchen scissors and began cutting his hair. He was so mad," Charlotte said laughing.

Sarah laughed and looked at Tim.

"You cut it down to nothing on the one side and I had to get my head buzzed," Tim said offensively.

Sarah laughed harder.

"Now that I have to see," she said.

"All photo evidence of that has been erased," Tim said, smiling at Sarah.

"That's not true. If you ever come to Kalamazoo, Sarah, I think we have photos of it somewhere," Charlotte said.

Tim gave his niece a look. Sarah laughed.

"What's your favorite memory of Uncle Tim?" Charlotte asked Sarah.

"Well, I haven't known him as long as you. So I don't have as many," Sarah responded.

"That's OK. What's your favorite?" she insisted.

Sarah thought back on all of her memories of Tim, from meeting him in the waiting room at her dad's appointments to the few dates they shared. If she was being honest, her favorite memory would have to be their first kiss on the couch at the bookstore. But she wasn't about to divulge that information to a 13-year-old.

"I would have to say the time I beat him at Battleship," Sarah said, winking at Tim.

"Whoa, whoa, whoa. If I remember correctly, I won that game," Tim said.

"Uncle Tim, it's Sarah's memory. If she said she won, then she won," Charlotte interrupted.

Sarah laughed.

"Actually, your uncle is right. He won that game. I just wanted to rile him up," she said.

"I like to do that too," Charlotte said laughing.

"Great. Now I have two girls who gang up on me," Tim said.

"Don't be a party pooper, Uncle Tim. It's all fun and games," Charlotte said.

"Yeah, Hoosier Tim," Sarah said jokingly.

Sarah and Charlotte both laughed.

"Is that how you two want to play?" Tim asked.

Sarah and Charlotte both nodded. Tim reached his hand over the side of the boat and began splashing water at the two of them. They threw their arms up to try to block the water from hitting their face, but Tim kept splashing them. He finally stopped after the two girls were drenched. All three of them were laughing.

Sarah and Charlotte looked at each other.

"Shall we?" Sarah asked.

"We shall," Charlotte replied.

Sarah and Charlotte made their way to where Tim was sitting.

"What are you two doing?" he asked.

Sarah and Charlotte struggled, but managed to pick Tim up.

"Put me down," he said laughing.

They carried him to the side of the boat and threw him overboard. Charlotte was laughing so hard she snorted, which caused her to laugh louder. Sarah was laughing too.

"Great. Now how am I supposed to get back in the boat?" Tim asked.

Sarah leaned over the side of the boat and reached her hand out to Tim.

"Here, let me help you," she said.

Tim grabbed her hand and pretended to pull himself up, but instead, he pulled her into the water with him.

"Tim!" Sarah exclaimed, splashing water at him.

The two of them laughed as they treaded the water.

"I think I'm going to stay onboard," Charlotte said laughing.

"If you change your mind, we'll be over here swimming," Tim said as he began to swim away from the boat.

Sarah followed. Charlotte pulled out a book and went to the front of the boat to read. She had her back turned towards Sarah and Tim. Tim made his way towards Sarah until they were inches apart. He eyed the boat to make sure Charlotte wasn't looking.

Tim leaned forward and kissed Sarah. She kissed him back. He pushed his tongue into her mouth and she slid hers over it into his mouth. She wrapped her legs around his waist, and they went under water for a minute before they both used their arms to bring themselves back to the surface.

"Oops," she said, as she started to remove her legs.

"No, it's OK. I got us," Tim said, pulling her legs back.

Tim put one hand on Sarah's butt and used the other to keep them afloat. Sarah put both of her hands behind Tim's neck and kissed him again. She pulled on his upper lip with her lips and then entered her tongue into his mouth. She kept kissing him like that until Tim started gasping for air. He removed his hand from her butt and used both arms to tread water.

"I think I need to get back on the boat. My arms are exhausted," he said sheepishly.

Sarah removed herself from Tim and treaded on her own.

"That's OK," she said with a smile.

He moved towards her and kissed her one more time on the lips. He gave her a wink and the two of them swam back towards the boat. Tim moved to the back of the boat and pulled a ladder down into the water.

"You knew how to get back on the boat this whole time?" Sarah asked.

Tim smiled at her.

"Yup. I just wanted to get you in here with me," he said.

Sarah laughed and splashed him one last time. Tim helped her up the ladder before climbing aboard himself. Sarah's white shirt was now completely see-through and showed her nude bra. She caught Tim staring at her chest. He blushed and looked away.

"I brought some towels," he said, moving towards his bag.

He pulled out a towel and wrapped it around Sarah's shoulders.

"Thanks," she said, giving him a smile.

He returned the smile and then grabbed a towel for himself. He looked towards the front of the boat at Charlotte. She was lost in her book, completely oblivious to the world around her.

"A good book will do that," Sarah said, following his gaze.

"Well, do you want to come to my place then?" Tim asked.

Sarah gave Tim a look.

"I didn't mean it like that. I just meant we could go back to my house and I could get you into some dry clothes," he said smiling.

Sarah had dry clothes in her car, but she liked the idea of going to Tim's house. She had never been there before. She was also intrigued at the idea of what might happen there. She and Tim had never done anything more than kiss and they had been on a few dates now. She was ready for that next step. She moved her gaze to Charlotte. Taking that next step would be hard with Tim's niece at the house, she thought.

"Charlotte mainly hangs out in her room when we're home," Tim said, almost reading Sarah's thoughts.

Sarah smiled at Tim.

"OK," she said. "We can go back to your house."

Tim smiled like a child on the last day of school before being let out for summer vacation. He pulled the anchor up and turned the boat back on. The sound of the motor brought Charlotte back to the real world. She turned and looked at Sarah and Tim and smiled.

"Are you ready to go home?" Tim asked.

Charlotte nodded.

"Is it OK if Sarah comes over for a little bit?" he asked.

"Of course," Charlotte said, smiling at Sarah.

Tim drove the boat back to the dock and returned the key. Sarah got into her car and followed Charlotte and Tim to his house. It was about a 10 minute drive from the park. Tim lived in a nice, two-story house in a new subdivision just outside the city limits.

"Wow. This looks nice," she said as she got out of her car.

"Thanks. I moved in about a year ago," Tim replied.

Tim led Sarah inside.

"I'll be in my room reading if you guys need me," Charlotte said before walking away.

"I told you," Tim said, winking at Sarah.

She let out a light laugh and waited by the front door while Tim grabbed her some dry clothes to change into. A few moments later he came back with a T-shirt and a pair of boxers.

"This is the only thing I could find that would probably fit you," he said.

Sarah laughed.

"This will work," she said, taking the clothes.

She slipped inside the bathroom by the entrance way and changed. Afterwards, Tim gave her a tour of the house. It had four bedrooms, two-and-a-half bathrooms, a kitchen, a laundry room, a dining room, a living room, and a three seasons room overlooking the backyard.

"Do you want something to drink?" Tim asked after the tour.

"Sure. I'll have whatever you're having," she said.

"OK. You can make yourself comfortable in the back room and I'll be in shortly," he said.

"OK," Sarah said.

She made her way to the three seasons room, which had a couch, a coffee table, two white wooden rocking chairs, an end table, and a bookshelf full of books and board games. Sarah sat in the middle of the couch. Shortly after, Tim walked in with two glasses of wine. He handed Sarah a glass and took a seat next to her on the couch.

"This is nice," she said, looking out the window into his yard.

Tim had a big fenced in backyard. There was a patio with a hot tub, and in the middle of his yard there was an in-ground fire pit with six wooden chairs around it.

"Thanks," he said. "This is my favorite room."

"I can see why," Sarah said, taking a sip of the wine.

Tim took a drink of his wine and then set the glass on the table. He put an arm around Sarah's shoulders.

"So what would you like to do?" he asked.

You, she answered in her head. But instead, she smiled up at him.

"It doesn't matter to me," she said.

"Well, we can play a game. Or we can pick up where we left off in the lake," he said suggestively.

"I like the second option," Sarah said, putting her glass on the table.

"Well, for starters, I think you were all over me," Tim said, pulling Sarah towards him.

"Was I?" Sarah asked.

"Mhm," Tim replied.

Sarah climbed onto Tim's lap, resting a leg on either side of him. She looked down at him and smiled.

"This brings back memories," he said, putting one hand on her waist and the other behind her neck.

He pulled her neck towards him and kissed her on the mouth, pushing his tongue inside. She moved both of her hands to his neck and slid her tongue around his. With his hand on her waist, Tim moved her hips back and forth in a humping motion. He moved his mouth to her neck where he grabbed a small portion of the skin with his lips and gave it a light suck. Sarah let out a soft moan.

Tim lifted the T-shirt over Sarah's head, exposing her bare breasts. He moved his hand from her neck down to her breasts and lightly grabbed one. He began massaging it with his fingers. Sarah removed Tim's shirt and eyed his abdomen. He was fit, but he wasn't built like Charlie, she thought. She quickly pushed Charlie out of her head and focused on Tim.

Tim maneuvered Sarah so her back was on the couch and he was on top of her. He lightly kissed her lips and began kissing his way down her body. He stopped briefly at her breasts and put one of her nipples in his mouth, giving it a light suck. Sarah moaned quietly. He continued his way down her body until he reached the boxers. He slowly pulled those down past her knees and off her feet. He kissed his way up from her ankle to her entrance.

He slid his tongue from her opening up to her clitoris. He placed it in his mouth and lightly sucked on it. Sarah arched her back and moaned. Tim released her clit from his mouth and slid his tongue back down to her opening. He traced his tongue around it a few times before he slipped it inside. Sarah moaned again.

He moved his tongue in and out, slowly at first. Then he began to move it faster, thrusting his tongue as far as he could inside of Sarah. She pulled a pillow over her face to muffle her moans. She wanted Tim. She tried to pull him up so they could continue to the next base, but he ignored her. He kept his tongue inside of her. He moved one of his hands up to

Sarah's clitoris and gently began to rub it with his thumb.

Sarah arched her back again. She held the pillow over her mouth and moaned loudly into it. Sarah was breathing heavy and her legs went numb. She was filled with a sensation she had never felt before. Tim slowly removed his tongue, lifted his head up, and wiped his mouth with his hand. Sarah was too exhausted to speak. She laid there in complete disbelief.

Tim smiled down at her. He made his way to her side and laid down next to her, resting an arm across her chest. Sarah still didn't move. She was trying to catch her breath. Tim let out a laugh. Sarah turned her head to face him with her mouth still open. He leaned over and kissed her on the forehead.

"Wow," Sarah said.

Tim laughed again.

"I never felt that way before," she said.

"I figured," Tim said.

"How?" Sarah asked, looking at him.

"Well, you were impatient to get to the next step. There's something beautiful and sensually pleasing about taking your time. It's not a race," he said.

"Oh," Sarah said, slightly embarrassed.

"That was your first?" he asked.

"My first what?" she asked.

"Your first orgasm," Tim replied.

"Oh. I mean, I guess so. I assumed I had them before, but it definitely never felt like that," she said, smiling at him. "That was incredible."

"Well, I'm happy to do it any time," he said, smiling back.

"Don't say that. I might take you up on that," she said laughing.

"Please do," he said, kissing her on the lips.

"But what about you?" she asked.

"What about me?" he asked.

"You don't get any pleasure from that," Sarah replied.

"Your reaction was pleasure enough. I'll take a raincheck on me," he said, giving Sarah a wink.

Sarah laughed and rolled on her side so she was facing Tim.

"I like you," she said.

"I like you too," he replied. "A lot."

Sarah smiled. She closed her eyes.

"Don't fall asleep," Tim said.

"I'm not. I'm just resting my eyes," Sarah said.

Tim laughed. He shook her slightly until she opened her eyes.

"You have to go home, Sarah," he said.

"I don't want to," she whined.

He laughed again.

"I don't want you to either, but I also don't want you to spend the night with Charlotte here. She might get the wrong idea," he said.

"Or the right idea," Sarah said playfully.

Tim laughed.

"I'll take a raincheck on that too," he said, giving Sarah another wink.

"Fine. I'll go," Sarah said, sitting up.

"You can keep the clothes," Tim said, handing Sarah the T-shirt.

She put the shirt back on and looked around for the boxers. Tim reached down and grabbed those and handed them to Sarah.

"Thanks," she said.

Sarah stood up to put them back on, but Tim stopped her by grabbing her hips. He lightly kissed her vagina and then let go of her hips. Sarah blushed and slowly pulled the boxers up.

"I'll walk you out," Tim said.

17

Sarah had been hoping Charlie wasn't going to be home, but when she saw his car in the driveway she knew that wasn't going to be the case. She knew he was already going to be mad at her for seeing Tim and that was without knowing anything had happened between them. She walked into her house still wearing Tim's clothes. Charlie was sitting on the couch in the living room watching TV.

He didn't turn around when she shut the door. So she quickly went upstairs to change before he saw her. She already knew they were going to have a fight, and if he saw her wearing Tim's boxers that would only make it worse. She had just entered her bedroom when she heard footsteps coming up the stairs.

"What the fuck, Sarah," Charlie said, clearly upset.

Sarah turned around to see him standing in her doorway.

"What?" Sarah asked, playing dumb.

"You're wearing his fucking clothes. His fucking underwear. Did you fuck him too?" he asked.

Sarah looked down at the clothes she had on.

"No. My clothes got wet on the boat ride and Tim gave me these to wear so I wouldn't have to drive home in wet clothes," Sarah said.

Charlie just stared at Sarah.

"You didn't have sex with him?" he asked.

"No," Sarah replied.

It technically wasn't a lie, she thought to herself.

"His niece was with us, Charlie," she said, trying to get off the topic of sex.

"Oh," Charlie said, looking towards the floor. "I forgot."

"Now if you don't mind, I'm going to shower and get ready for bed," she said.

Charlie didn't say anything. Sarah walked past him and into the bathroom where she locked the door, which was something she never did. But in that moment she did not want to see Charlie. She stepped into the shower and let the hot water run over her naked body for a moment. She closed her eyes and pictured Tim going down on her. She opened her eyes and decided she had to see Tim again.

After thoroughly rinsing all of the lake water smell off of herself, Sarah exited the shower and dried off. She put pajamas on and went into her bedroom where Charlie was sitting on the bed. She could tell he was clearly upset. She slowly walked towards him and sat down next to him.

"I'm not OK with this, Sarah," Charlie said, looking at her with pain in his eyes.

"With what?" Sarah asked, playing dumb again.

"With you seeing Tim. I can't fucking do this. I can't have you go out and see another guy and then come home and play fucking house with me. That's not fair to me," he said.

"I agree," Sarah said, placing a hand on Charlie's knee.

"They why did you do it?" Charlie asked.

"Because I like Tim. And I'm not going to stop seeing him, Charlie. I'm sorry, but I'm not," she said, pulling her hand back.

"So what does that mean for us?" Charlie asked.

"Well for starters, I think you should start staying at your apartment again," she said slowly.

"You're the one who asked me to stay here," he said defensively.

"I know. And I am really appreciative of you staying here and helping me through the funeral and everything. I am so thankful you were here for that. I honestly don't know how I could have gotten through that without you," she said, looking at Charlie.

Charlie looked towards the floor and put his face in his hands.

"I know we've had some fun these past few weeks and I don't know if anything will be able to go back to the way it was before we had sex, but I really miss my best friend, Charlie," Sarah said.

Charlie lifted his head up and looked at Sarah.

"How am I supposed to go from being your lover to your best friend again?" Charlie asked.

"I don't know, but I would like us to try," she responded.

"I'm in love with you, Sarah. Don't you know that?" he asked.

"I know, but I don't feel the same way. I mean, I love you too, but not the same way you love me," she said.

"Jesus Christ, Sarah. Then what the fuck have we been doing these past few weeks?" he asked, standing up.

"I don't know," Sarah replied, looking up at him.

Charlie began to pace back and forth across Sarah's bedroom floor.

"I don't know if I can go back to how things were before," he said, looking at Sarah.

"Can we at least try?" Sarah asked.

"That's what you want? You want to throw away everything that happened these past few weeks and just pretend it never happened?" he asked.

"We don't have to pretend it never happened. I just want my best friend back," she said.

"I'm going to need some time, Sarah. You're fucking breaking my heart right now," Charlie said, grabbing the back of a chair for support.

"I never wanted to hurt you, Charlie. But I don't feel the same way about you and that's not fair to either of us," she said, getting up to stand next to Charlie.

She placed one hand on his back and the other on one of his hands, which was still holding the chair. Charlie turned around and wrapped Sarah up into a hug. She hugged him back. The two of them stood in silence for what felt like an eternity to Sarah. Finally, Charlie released her and took a step back.

"The promise I made your dad, he made me promise him that I would always make you happy. I don't know how to do that if I'm not with you. But if this is what you want, and if you think Tim will make you happy, then I'll try," Charlie said.

Sarah gave Charlie a half-smile.

"I don't know if Tim will make me happy or if he is the one for me, or if there even is one person out there for everyone. But I want to explore that option and see what comes from it," Sarah said.

"I understand. I certainly don't like the idea, but I understand it," Charlie said.

They stood in silence for a moment looking at each other.

"I'll always be here for you, Sarah. But right now, I'm going to need some space. I'll be in touch when I'm ready to talk or hangout or whatever it is you want to do," he said.

He stepped forward and hugged Sarah one more time. She held him tight and rested her head on his shoulder. She was going to miss Charlie. In her heart, she knew things would never be the same between them. Charlie let go of Sarah.

"Well, I'll pack up my things and head home," he said.

"I'll help," Sarah said with a half-smile.

Sarah helped Charlie pack up the few things he had at her house. She walked him to the front door. Charlie dropped his bag on the ground and grabbed both of Sarah's hands. He gave her a half-smile.

"I know," she said. "I'm going to miss you, Cha-Cha."

"I'm going to miss you too, Sare-bear," he replied.

18

The next morning, Sarah felt weird waking up alone. She had gotten use to sleeping next to Charlie and it gave her a sense of comfort. She longed for that feeling again, but she knew she couldn't invite him back. She had been using him to avoid feeling alone in a house that now felt empty.

As she laid in bed contemplating how much time she had before she had to get up to get ready for work, her phone let out a ping. She got out of bed and walked over to the phone. It was a text message from Tim.

Good morning! Charlotte and I had a lot of fun yesterday. Thanks for coming. Tomorrow is her last night with me before I drive her back to K-Zoo on Saturday. I'm going to make tacos for dinner and she asked if you would join us. I don't want you to feel obligated to, but it would be nice to see you again, the text read.

Sarah smiled. After the night prior, she could not wait to see Tim again. Especially now that Charlie was out of the picture.

I love tacos. I'm in! What time should I get to your house? she texted back.

Let's say 6. We'll see you then, Tim texted back with a kissing emoji.

Perfect, she replied, with another kissing emoji.

Thursday dragged on as Sarah impatiently waited for her dinner date with Tim. She was stocking books at the shop as she thought about it. Was it really a date though, she thought to herself. In Charlotte's terms it was, she decided.

She counted all of their dates in her head. If she was going by Charlotte's definition of a date, this would be their seventh date. And they still haven't done the deed, she thought to herself. She wanted to so bad, but she knew that wasn't going to happen with Charlotte there. She pulled out her phone and re-read Tim's text message. It said he was driving her home Saturday.

Sarah did a quick internet search to see how far of a drive it was from Muncie to Kalamazoo. It was about three hours. She did the math in her head and decided after visiting time and everything, Tim would be gone about eight hours. If he left in the morning, she could see him at night and they could finally have sex, she thought. Sarah's heart started beating faster thinking about it.

The rest of the day was a blur. Sarah did not sleep much that night because she was too excited to see Tim. When her alarm went off Friday morning to get up for work, Sarah jumped out of bed. She raced to her closet to find something to wear for the night. She picked out a floral yellow summer dress. She grabbed a brown cardigan to wear over it to make it work appropriate.

Sarah's work day seemed to prolong itself. It was only made worse by the fact that she had to work half of her shift with Cindy. Cindy had been picking up more hours since she wasn't taking summer classes. So Sarah ended up working with her more than she would like. That day though, Cindy kept asking questions about Sarah's "two boyfriends."

"They're not my boyfriends," Sarah responded.

"Well, whatever they are, how is that going?" Cindy asked.

"Cindy, I am your manager. These are inappropriate questions to be asking," Sarah said.

"Oh," Cindy said, becoming embarrassed. "I'm sorry."

Cindy walked into the back room and Sarah thought it looked like she might start crying. She rolled her eyes and let it be. Sarah continued working in the front of the store until it was time for her to leave. She went into the back room to tell Cindy she was leaving for the day.

"OK," Cindy said, not looking at Sarah.

Sarah knew something was bothering Cindy, but she wasn't going to dive into that when she had somewhere to go. She ignored Cindy's short response.

"OK. See you later," Sarah said as she left the room.

Sarah had an hour to spare before she was supposed to be at Tim's house. She decided to drive to the cemetery to visit her dad's grave. It was something she hadn't done since the funeral. She wasn't a religious person and she didn't believe in spirits, so she knew her dad wasn't spiritually at the gravesite. But it was something he used to do for her mom, so she thought it might be nice to do the same for him.

Sarah stopped at a flower shop on the way and bought a bouquet of calla lilies. She took the flowers to the cemetery and placed them on the grave. To her surprise, there was another freshly placed bouquet of calla lilies on the grave. Charlie, she thought to herself. She wondered how often Charlie had been out to her dad's grave, but she quickly pushed him out of her head.

She sat down on the grass next to the grave. In front of the headstone, there was still a lot of dirt from the burial just a week prior. Sarah couldn't believe it had only been a week. It felt like an eternity had passed since she buried her father. She rested her back against the side of the stone.

She closed her eyes so she could be fully present in that moment. She focused on her other senses. She placed her hands on the ground to feel the grass. It was a little itchy and nearing time to be cut. Sarah felt the heat of the sun on her skin. It felt nice, she thought. She could hear birds chirping in the background. They weren't singing, just talking to each other, she decided.

Besides the sound of the birds, it was silent. Sarah found it peaceful. She breathed in through her nose to smell her surroundings. She got a light hint of the calla lilies she brought. She opened her eyes and looked around. There wasn't anyone else at the cemetery. She was alone. But she didn't feel alone. For the first time since before Edward died, Sarah felt at peace.

She looked at the time on her phone and realized it was time to head to Tim's house. She stood up and looked at her parent's grave one more time. She smiled at it. She didn't know how, but for some reason she suddenly knew she was going to be OK. She was happy she made the detour to the cemetery. It was just what she needed to move on, she thought to herself.

Sarah arrived to Tim's house, almost feeling like a new woman. She felt relaxed, confident, and maybe even happy. It had been a long time since she truly felt happiness, even before Edward was diagnosed with cancer. But she liked this new feeling she was experiencing. She walked up to the door and rang the doorbell.

"I'll get it," she heard Charlotte shout from inside.

A few seconds later, the door opened to Charlotte's smiling face.

"Sarah!" Charlotte exclaimed, giving Sarah a hug.

"Hi, Charlotte," Sarah said, returning the hug.

"I hope you're hungry. Dinner is just about ready," Charlotte said, leading Sarah inside.

The two of them walked into the kitchen where Tim was putting all of the food out on the island. He stopped what he was doing when they entered. He turned towards them with a smile on his face.

"Hello, beautiful," he said to Sarah.

Tim walked across the room and put his arms around Sarah's lower back. He leaned down and kissed her lightly on the lips.

"Ooh," Charlotte said teasingly.

Tim pulled his head back. He and Sarah smiled at each other.

"Hello," Sarah said.

"Wow," he said looking at her.

"What?" Sarah asked.

"You are just glowing today," he said.

Sara blushed.

"You're not too bad yourself," Sarah said, winking at Tim.

"OK guys, don't make me barf," Charlotte said.

Sarah and Tim laughed.

"Alright, ladies," Tim said, walking towards the island. "Dinner is ready."

"I'm so hungry," Charlotte said dramatically.

Charlotte began fixing her plate and Sarah and Tim followed. There were hard shells, soft shells, ground beef, shredded chicken, shredded cheese, lettuce, tomatoes, onions, sour cream, salsa, and rice.

"You really went all out," Sarah said, while fixing her plate.

"Only the best for my girls," Tim said.

Sarah smiled at him. He returned the gesture. The three of them sat down at the kitchen table to eat their tacos. They would laugh whenever one of them made a mess, since tacos aren't the cleanest food to eat.

"I love tacos," Charlotte said, after she finished off her last one.

"Me too," Tim said, winking at Sarah.

Sarah blushed and looked down at her now-empty plate. She pictured Tim going down on her again and felt her breathing accelerate.

"What about you, Sarah?" Charlotte asked.

"I'm sorry, what?" Sarah asked, coming back to the present.

Tim chuckled to himself.

"Do you like tacos?" Charlotte asked.

"Yeah, they're good," Sarah responded, smiling at Tim.

"Well, if everyone is done, I'll put the food away," Tim said.

"Yeah, I'm stuffed," Charlotte responded.

"Me too," Sarah said.

"OK. You two can put your plates in the sink and I'll wash them later," Tim said, standing up.

Sarah and Charlotte carried the dirty dishes to the sink while Tim put the leftovers away. Sarah went to go take a seat by the island, but Charlotte interrupted her.

"So Sarah, Uncle Tim tells me you like to play games," she said.

"Yeah, I love them," Sarah replied, smiling at Charlotte.

"Do you want to play one?" Charlotte asked.

"Sure! What game do you want to play?" Sarah asked.

"How about Clue?" Charlotte asked.

"I love Clue," Sarah replied.

"You two can go get it set up in the back room and I'll be in there in a minute," Tim said, smiling at them.

"I call dibs on Miss Scarlet," Charlotte said as she led Sarah to the three seasons room.

"That's fine. I'll be Mrs. Peacock," Sarah said, taking a seat on the couch.

Charlotte grabbed Clue from Tim's game collection and carried it to the coffee table.

"I'll be Professor Plum," Tim called out from the kitchen.

Sarah placed all of the game pieces on the board while Charlotte shuffled the cards and dealt them out. Tim walked into the room just as Charlotte finished dealing the cards. The three of them took turns entering rooms and making accusations as they marked off clues on their checklist. Tim was the first one to make the final accusation, but he had it wrong so he was out of the game. Charlotte made her final guess right after Tim lost. She had all three items correct. It was Mrs. White in the Kitchen with the knife.

"I was so close," Sarah said.

"Sorry losers, maybe next time," Charlotte said laughing.

Sarah and Tim looked at each other and laughed.

"Well you know what they say, losers have to clean up," Charlotte said as she stood up. "I'm going to go get all of my things together for tomorrow. I'll be upstairs if you need me. If I don't see you before you leave, Sarah, it was nice meeting you."

"It was nice meeting you too, Charlotte. I hope you enjoy the rest of your summer," Sarah said.

Charlotte left the room and they heard her walk upstairs. Sarah and Tim smiled at each other as they packed the game back up in its box. Tim put the game back on the shelf and took a seat next to Sarah on the couch.

"Here we are again," he said, smiling at Sarah.

Sarah smiled back at him and leaned in to kiss him. Their lips met and Sarah had planned to pull away, but it felt as though there was a magnetic force pulling their lips together. She kept kissing him. Tim leaned back, pulling Sarah down with him so they were laying side by side on the couch.

While still kissing, Tim pulled Sarah's body on top of him. He put his hands on her hips and pulled them in a humping motion. Sarah started dry humping him while her tongue was still in his mouth. She could feel him growing hard beneath his jeans. She moved her lips to his neck.

"I want you," she whispered in his ear.

"I want you too, but we have to wait," he replied.

Sarah stopped humping him and propped herself up so she could look into his eyes.

"How long?" she asked.

"How about tomorrow night after I get back?" Tim asked.

Sarah smiled and leaned down and kissed him without tongue. She rolled to the side of him. Tim turned to his side to face her.

"Tomorrow works for me," she said.

Tim lightly traced her lips with his fingers.

"You can come over and I'll make us some cocktails," he said, slowly tracing his fingers down her neck.

"We could strip down to nothing and take a soak in the hot tub," he said, gliding his fingers over her breasts and down her stomach.

"I like hot tubs," Sarah said.

"We can turn the jets on for a nice massage," Tim said as he slid his fingers under her dress and up towards her underwear.

"Mmm. That sounds nice," she said as her breathing accelerated.

Tim slowly pulled her panties down just a little to give him access to her opening.

"Then I could enter you as we stare up at the stars with warm water surrounding us," he said as he thrusted his index finger inside her.

Sarah opened her mouth and let out a soft moan. Tim moved his finger in and out of her slowly. Then he pulled it out and thrusted his index and middle finger inside her. Sarah moaned again. She wrapped her arms around Tim's neck and forced her tongue in his mouth. Tim kept fingering her, moving his fingers back and forth, faster and faster.

Sarah was so wet. She could hear his fingers sliding against her wetness. She would usually be embarrassed by that, but the pleasure was too good. She could feel her face go numb. She stopped kissing Tim and moaned softly in his ear. Her back arched and she bit down on Tim's shoulder. Then her body relaxed.

Tim removed his fingers from Sarah's vagina. She leaned back against the back of the couch, completely out of breath. Tim smiled at her. He leaned down and kissed her forehead. She wanted to say something, but words wouldn't come out. Tim let out a light giggle.

"I'm going to wash my hands and I'll be right back," he said, winking at Sarah.

Tim left the room. Sarah managed to sit up on the couch and pull her underwear back up. She looked at her reflection in the window and quickly brushed her hair with her fingers. She replayed that moment in her head. She had never been fingered like that before. Usually it was just a quick event before the main event, but that was incredible, she thought. Tim was right, she added, there was something sensually satisfying about taking your time.

Since he was so great at foreplay, Sarah couldn't wait to see what Tim was like in bed. That scene he described in the hot tub sounded amazing to her. Tim walked back in as Sarah was picturing the two of them in the hot tub. She just smiled at him and shook her head.

"What?" he asked, smiling.

"Just wow. That's all I can say," she said.

He laughed and joined her on the couch. Tim placed his arm around Sarah's shoulders.

"I mean, it's no Thailand, but I'm trying to stand out against the competition," he said, looking at Sarah.

Sarah laughed.

"There's no competition," she said.

"Really?" Tim asked, raising an eyebrow towards her.

"Really," she replied.

"Well good. Then I can start being selfish," he said, winking at Sarah.

"I guess I'll have to step up my game tomorrow to crush my competition," Sarah said jokingly.

"Good luck. That's a tough competition," Tim said seriously.

"What?" Sarah asked, shocked.

She never thought about Tim dating other girls. She was too busy deciding between him and Charlie to even think he might be making the same decision with someone else. The thought of him with another woman saddened her.

"I'm just kidding," Tim said laughing.

Sarah looked at him.

"It was a joke. I promise," he said.

"Really?" she asked.

"Yes. You're the only girl I'm seeing," Tim said.

"Good," Sarah said, smiling.

"But now that you mention it. Do you want us to be exclusive?" Tim asked.

Sarah thought about it for a minute. If she said yes, she wouldn't be able to see anyone else. Which she wasn't interested in anyway at that point, she thought.

She wanted Tim and only Tim. She also didn't want Tim to see anyone else, she decided.

"Yeah, I would like that," she said.

Tim smiled.

"Me too," he said.

19

Saturday morning arrived and Sarah spent extra time getting ready for the day. She shaved her legs and trimmed up her lady bits. She curled her already curly hair and applied a light coat of make-up. She wanted everything to be perfect for her and Tim's first time together. She was excited and nervous to finally take this step with him.

Sarah wanted to wear something sexy for the big night, but she didn't like her lingerie options. She decided to go shopping for a new bra and underwear set. She wanted something lacey. She went to the mall and hit up the only lingerie store. They didn't have many options.

Sarah didn't have big breasts, so she liked to wear push-up bras to give her boobs a fuller look. The store didn't have any sexy push-up bras, Sarah decided. Instead, she bought a black lace bodysuit. It didn't give as much lift as Sarah would have preferred, but it gave a little lift. It would have to do, she determined.

While she was leaving the mall, Tim texted her that he was just leaving Kalamazoo. It was about 2 p.m. He told Sarah to meet him at his house around 5:30 p.m. That gave her three and a half hours to kill.

She went home and tried on her new lingerie. She stood in front of the full-length mirror in her bedroom and did different poses. She wanted to see what angle was the sexiest. After doing about a half a dozen poses, she went into her closet to find an outfit to wear over her bodysuit.

She thought just skinny jeans could be sexy. After trying them on, Sarah decided she looked like a prostitute. She took the jeans off and continued scouring through her clothes. She concluded she wanted something that would be easy to remove, which eliminated jeans.

She tried on a black bodycon dress, but you could see the outline of the lace on her bodysuit. Sarah removed the dress and continued searching through her clothes. She found a red slip dress in the back of her closet she had forgotten about. She tried that on and it was a perfect fit.

The only issue was the straps on the dress did not cover the straps from her bodysuit. It wasn't that big of an issue, but Sarah hated when her straps showed. She grabbed a black blazer to wear over the dress. Sexy and sophisticated, she thought to herself as she checked out her reflection in the mirror.

Sarah paced around the house until it was time for her to drive to Tim's house. The whole drive there, her hands were sweating and her heart was racing. She was super excited for what the night entailed, but for some reason she was extremely nervous. Sex never made her nervous before. She just usually went for it. But it was different with Tim.

She arrived to his house and quickly checked her breath, which was fine. She wiped her sweaty hands on her bare legs to dry them off and exited her car. She went up to the door and rang the doorbell. A short moment later, Tim answered the door.

He was wearing navy blue pants with a light blue button-up shirt. He had his sleeves rolled up to his elbows. He looks fucking sexy, Sarah thought to herself. She wanted to pin him against the wall right there and begin taking his clothes off, but she knew he didn't like to rush.

"Wow," Tim said, smiling at her.

"Back atcha," she said, examining his body.

Tim grabbed Sarah's hand and led her inside the house. He closed the door and leaned down to kiss her lightly on the lips. Her heart was beating so fast. Tim pulled away and led Sarah to the kitchen where he had prepared a mini bar on the island. He had a blender with some type of frozen pink drink inside, a few different bottles of wine, some rum and an unopened bottle of tequila.

"What would you like?" Tim asked.

"What's in the blender?" Sarah asked.

"Strawberry daiquiris," he replied.

"Ooh! I will start with one of those, please," she said.

"Good choice," Tim said as he walked towards the blender.

Tim poured the mixture into two cocktail glasses and garnished it with a little umbrella.

"Here you go, my lady," he said, handing one of the glasses to Sarah.

"Thank you," she responded, taking a drink. "Mmm. This is delicious."

"I'm glad you like it," Tim replied, taking a drink of his.

Sarah flashed him a smile.

"Do you want to sit outside, or head into the back room, or go someplace else?" he asked as his eyes trailed up the stairs towards his bedroom.

Sarah followed his gaze.

"I've never been in your bedroom," she said intrigued.

"OK. Bedroom it is," Tim said with a smile.

With his free hand, Tim grabbed Sarah's hand and led her up the stairs to his bedroom. It was a large master suite with a king size bed, a large dresser, two end tables, a walk-in closet, and a connecting bathroom.

"This is nice," Sarah said, turning around to face Tim.

"Thank you," he said as he grabbed her glass and placed it on top of his dresser next to his.

He took a step towards Sarah and placed his hands on her hips. She wrapped her arms around his neck. Tim leaned down and placed his lips on hers. He gently pulled her upper lip with his lips and then slid his tongue inside her mouth. Sarah tightened her grip around Tim's neck and glided her tongue over his.

While still kissing, Tim moved his hands up Sarah's body and pulled her blazer off of her arms. He dropped it on the floor. Sarah moved her hands down his torso to his waist where she undid his belt. She pulled it off and dropped it next to her blazer. Tim took a few steps towards the bed, moving Sarah with him. He stopped when her hips hit the front of the bed.

He took a step back and began unbuttoning his shirt while eying Sarah's body. She sat down at the foot of the bed and removed her heels, never taking her eyes off of Tim. He undid the last button and bit his lip as he slowly removed his shirt. Sarah kept his gaze and scooted backwards on the bed. Tim followed, crawling on top of her.

Sarah rolled Tim over and climbed on top of him. She kissed him hard on the mouth and then moved her way down his chest, leaving behind a trail of kisses. She stopped when she got to his pants. She undid the button and then slowly pulled down the zipper while smiling at Tim. He smiled back and placed his hands behind his head.

Sarah pulled Tim's pants all the way down his legs and he kicked them off. He was wearing black boxers with colorful ice cream cones on them. Sarah was surprised. She thought he would have been a briefs man, but she continued her mission. She pulled his underwear down to reveal a semi-hard penis that was already about 5-6 inches if she had to guess.

She bent down and gently kissed his thigh, making her way up to his manhood. Sarah grabbed it with one hand and gave it a light stroke before she placed it in her mouth. She slid her mouth as far down as she could without gagging and slowly brought it back up. She continued that motion while wrapping her tongue around his shaft.

Tim's penis grew harder and longer in her mouth. She could only fit about half of it in her mouth by the time is was fully erect. She used her hand to stroke the bottom half as she worked the top with her mouth and tongue. Tim moaned, which gave Sarah motivation to keep going. Her hand and mouth were synchronized and she moved them faster. Tim moaned again.

He grabbed her arms and pulled her up towards him. Tim grabbed the bottom of her dress and pulled it up over her head. He tossed it to the side of the bed. He looked at her bodysuit confused.

"I'll get it," Sarah said slightly embarrassed.

She sat up on her knees and pulled the straps down her arms. She shimmied the bodysuit down to her hips. She rolled onto her back to pull it down her legs, but Tim took over. He leaned over her and removed it the rest of the way. He climbed back over her body and gave her a light kiss on the lips.

He lightly kissed his way down her body, just grazing her skin. Sarah could feel her breathing accelerate. When he reached her vagina, he gently flicked her clitoris with his tongue. Sarah let out a moan. He continued down to her opening where it was already wet. He thrusted his tongue inside her, slowly at first. Then he moved it in and out aggressively. Sarah moaned louder.

She wanted Tim. She didn't want to wait anymore. She grabbed his arms and pulled him up towards her. He climbed over her naked body and smiled at her. He reached over to his bedside table and pulled out a condom. He sat up and quickly rolled it over his still-erect penis.

He leaned back down and guided the tip of his penis inside Sarah with his hand. She let out a soft moan. Tim kissed her neck and pushed a few inches deeper. She moaned again. He pulled back a few inches and then dove further inside. Sarah moaned again. She wrapped her arms around Tim's back.

Tim thrusted in and out of her, moving harder and faster. Sarah's legs began to tremble, but he kept going. He was breathing harder, while Sarah was practically screaming in pleasure. Tim performed one last thrust before he collapsed on Sarah. They were both out of breath.

They laid there in silence. Then Tim propped himself up on his elbows, gave Sarah a quick kiss, and then retreated into the bathroom. Sarah laid in bed replaying their lovemaking in her head. With all of her previous lovers, she had to tell them "harder" or "faster." But she didn't have to with Tim. He knew how to hit all of her spots, she thought to herself.

Tim returned to the bed with both of their daiquiris in his hand. He was still naked and Sarah was impressed by the size of his manhood in its natural state. He smiled and handed Sarah's drink to her. Then he quickly sucked his down. Sarah didn't realize how thirsty she was until she took a drink. She sucked hers right down too. Tim laughed.

"Exercise makes you thirsty," he said, grabbing her glass.

"That's my favorite kind of exercise," Sarah said, laying back down on the bed.

"Oh yeah?" Tim asked as he placed the glasses on his bedside table.

"Mhm," Sarah said, smiling at him.

Tim crawled over the bed to Sarah and laid his head on her bare chest.

"Mine too," he said.

Sarah wrapped her arm around Tim and held him close. Tim lifted his head and looked at Sarah.

"What?" she asked.

"You're very vocal in bed," he said with a grin.

"Sorry," Sarah said embarrassed.

"No, I like it. I just wasn't expecting it," he said. "It was a nice surprise."

"Oh," Sarah said, not sure if he was telling the truth.

"It tells me I'm doing something right. If you were quiet, I would assume you didn't like it and try to do something different," Tim said.

"You don't need to do anything different. You were perfect," she said matter-of-factly.

"You weren't half-bad yourself," he said, winking at Sarah.

Sarah grabbed one of Tim's pillows and hit him with it. He laughed.

"I'm just kidding," he said, taking the pillow away from Sarah.

She gave him a friendly glare. Her stomach rumbled. She realized she didn't eat dinner.

"Are you hungry?" Tim asked with a smile.

Sarah nodded her head. Tim stood up from the bed and picked Sarah up with his arms.

"What are you doing?" she asked laughing.

"Carrying you to the kitchen," he responded.

"You're not carrying me down stairs. Put me down," Sarah said.

"Nope," Tim said, carrying her out the bedroom door.

Tim took the first step downstairs and Sarah wrapped her arms around his back.

"Don't worry. I'm not going to drop you," he said laughing.

He carried her down the steps and into the kitchen where he put her down.

"Now, what would you like to eat?" he asked, opening the fridge.

Sarah walked up behind him, wrapped her arms around his waist and peeked her head around his torso.

"Tacos," she said as she spotted the leftovers from the night before.

"OK, tacos it is," Tim replied.

The two of them sat down and ate the leftover tacos. Afterwards, Sarah looked down at her still naked body and worried she might start to look bloated. Tim followed her gaze.

"You're beautiful," he said.

She blushed.

"You're not half-bad yourself," she said laughing.

Tim joined in the laughter.

"I deserve that one," he said smiling.

The light shining through the kitchen window caught Sarah's eye. She turned to look and noticed the sun was setting. The sky displayed a series of orange, purple and pink hues. Tim followed her gaze.

"Do you want to go sit in the hot tub?" he asked.

"I didn't bring a suit," she answered.

"That's fine," Tim said.

"What about your neighbors?" Sarah asked.

Tim laughed.

"I have a privacy fence. They won't see us," he said.

"Do you promise?" she asked.

"I promise," he replied.

"OK. That sounds nice," Sarah said.

Tim led Sarah outside to the patio. He opened up a plastic chest where he kept his towels and removed two of them. He carried them to the hot tub and set them on a bench next to it as he removed the cover to the hot tub. Steam rose up towards the sky. Sarah dipped her hand into the water.

"Wow, that feels nice," she said.

"Go ahead and get in," Tim said.

Sarah slowly stepped over the edge of the hot tub and gently lowered her naked body into the water. Tim walked over to his outside radio and turned on some slow jams. He walked back towards the hot tub and climbed in. He sat down next to Sarah and put his arm around her shoulder.

"This is nice," she said.

"Yeah, this is my second favorite nighttime activity," Tim said.

"What's your first?" Sarah asked.

Tim just smiled at her.

"Oh," she said laughing.

Tim leaned over and kissed her on the cheek. She turned her face towards him and kissed him gently on the lips. He kissed her back and slowly slid his tongue inside her mouth. Sarah grabbed his neck and thrusted her tongue into his mouth. Tim pulled her towards him so she was sitting on his lap facing him.

She could feel his penis grow beneath her. Sarah moved her lips to Tim's neck and gave it a light suck. He gripped her hips and moved them back and forth over his growing phallus. Sarah moved her lips up to Tim's ear and gave his lower earlobe a light nibble. He let out a soft moan in her ear.

He pulled Sarah down so his penis entered her vagina. She let out a loud moan. Tim covered her mouth with his hand.

"My neighbors might not be able to see you, but they can hear you," he said between breaths.

"Sorry," Sarah said embarrassed.

"It's OK, baby," he said. "Save your moans for the bedroom. I love them."

He kissed Sarah on the cheek and continued thrusting into her. She put her mouth on his shoulder and moaned quietly into his skin.

"There you go, baby," he said.

Sarah thrusted her hips against him. She moved harder and harder. She dug her nails into his back as she screamed with pleasure in her head. Tim tilted his head back and bit his tongue to hold back his moan. She continued to move back and forth over him until he quickly pulled her off of him. She looked at him confused.

"I'm sorry. I just don't want to take any chances," he said.

"It's OK. I'm on birth control," Sarah replied, making her way back towards Tim.

Tim placed his hand against Sarah's chest to halt her.

"That's not 100 percent effective, Sarah. I'd rather us be safe," he said.

"OK," Sarah said annoyed.

"Come here," Tim said, pulling Sarah on his lap. "I can still make you feel good."

20

Sarah and Tim quickly became inseparable after that night. They would spend the night together three to four times a week, going back and forth between both of their houses. Sarah preferred going to Tim's house because it was nicer and he had a hot tub. She also enjoyed sitting out by his fire pit at night, snacking on s'mores.

Before they knew it, it was the beginning of August and almost two months since their initial first date. Sarah wasn't one for celebrating monthiversaries, but Tim planned a weekend getaway to a cabin on a lake. Sarah was looking forward to their first adventure together. She hoped it was going to be the first of many for them.

She was alone at her house packing her bag for the weekend. She was about to pack some tampons in case she started her period when she realized she didn't have her period last month. She ran to her desk and quickly flipped open her calendar. It had been two months since her last period. Fuck, she thought to herself. Sarah had late periods in the past, but she never missed one.

She hadn't felt sick or anything, so she was hoping it was just a fluke. She knew she had to take a pregnancy test to calm her nerves. Sarah started taking deep breaths and told herself everything was going to be OK as she walked to her car. She drove to the pharmacy near her house and bought two separate tests.

Sarah didn't remember driving home from the pharmacy, but she found herself in her bathroom, peeing on one of the tests. She placed the test on the counter and had to wait two minutes for the result. She kept looking at the clock and time seemed to stand still for those two minutes. She began to breathe harder. She reminded herself to take deep breaths.

She looked at the clock again and it had been two minutes. She slowly walked to the counter and looked down at the test. Two lines were clearly displayed, which indicated she was pregnant. Sarah's body began to shake and she grabbed the edge of the counter for support. Tears welled in her eyes.

Sarah quickly opened the other test and forced herself to urinate on it. She placed it on the counter next to the first test and waited another two painstaking minutes. After what seemed like an eternity, she looked at the results. The test showed two lines. She punched the counter in anger.

She sunk down to the bathroom floor and began to sob. Her body was shaking. She wasn't ready to be a mom, she thought to herself. She didn't want to be a mom, at least not yet, she decided. Sarah didn't know what she was going to do.

Her thoughts were interrupted by a ping from her phone. Sarah wiped her tears on her hand and grabbed her phone. It was a text message from Tim.

I'm about to leave my house. Is there anything you want me to pick up on my way to get you?, the message read.

Tim was coming to get her for their romantic weekend away. Sarah had forgotten about the adventure they had planned. She knew she would not be able to enjoy the weekend after the news she just received, and she wasn't ready to tell Tim – or anybody for that matter. She knew she had to leave her house before Tim arrived. She quickly pulled herself off of the bathroom floor and rushed outside to her car.

She had no idea where she was going to go, she just knew she had to get away from there. She pulled out of her driveway and drove until she was outside of Muncie's city limits. She came across a park that had a hill overlooking the city. Sarah pulled into the parking lot. She sat inside her car for a few minutes, gripping her steering wheel. She couldn't believe this was happening to her.

She exited her car and walked towards the hill. She sat there in silence, replaying the timeline of events in her head. It had to be Charlie's, she confirmed to herself. Her last period was in the beginning of June and she and Tim didn't have sex until July. Fuck, she thought again.

Sarah had not talked to Charlie since the day he moved out of her house. Not even a single text message. For all she knew, Charlie probably hated her. She knew she broke his heart. She realized she never even reached out afterwards to see how he was doing. She was such a bad friend, she thought to herself.

She started to cry again, but quickly wiped away her tears. Darkness surrounded her and Sarah noticed it had become nighttime. She realized she must have been sitting on that hill for hours, but it didn't feel that long to her. She didn't move. Instead, she found herself staring off into the black abyss of the night sky.

She wondered how her life had become so complicated. She wished she could go back in time to a few months prior when her life was full of adventure. Before her dad was diagnosed with cancer. Before Charlie came home. Before she ever even met Tim. Sarah liked Tim, but they met because her dad was sick. If she could go back in time, she would choose a time when her dad was still healthy.

Sarah began to sob uncontrollably. She missed her dad. She realized she had been distracting herself with Tim to not think about him. But she missed him. She missed their talks. She missed their traditions. She even missed his vulgar, offensive language. She wanted to see him again.

She pulled herself up from the ground and walked back to her car. She pulled out of the park and began to drive to the cemetery. Tears kept pouring out of her eyes. She tried to wipe them away, but they kept coming down. Her vision became blurred.

Sarah must have crossed the centerline on the road because she heard a loud honk. She looked up to see bright lights coming right at her, and then everything went dark. She could hear sirens in the background and people talking, but she couldn't make out what they were saying. She tried to open her eyes, but was unable to. It stayed dark and the sirens and voices faded away.

Sarah had crossed the centerline right into the path of a semi-truck. It happened so fast the driver of the semi didn't have time to swerve. He honked his horn to alert Sarah, but it was too late. They collided head on. Sarah went unconscious almost immediately. Her body had to be extricated from her car, which was totaled in the collision.

First responders rushed her to the nearest hospital in an ambulance. She lost a lot of blood and had to have blood transfusions. Doctors hooked her up to all kinds of machines to keep her organs functioning. She was listed in extremely critical condition.

It took some time for the hospital to find a relative of Sarah's since Edward was still listed as her emergency contact. They went through Edward's file to find the number for Sarah's Aunt Susan. One of the nurses called her and told her what had happened. Susan then called Charlie to let him know. Susan didn't know Sarah and Charlie had a falling out, but it didn't even matter at that point.

Susan and Charlie both rushed to the hospital to see Sarah. Initially, the doctors wouldn't allow Charlie to see Sarah since he wasn't family, but Susan put him down on the list of people who were permitted to visit. Susan and Charlie walked into Sarah's hospital room. They both started crying when they saw her.

Sarah had a bandage wrapped around her head to control the bleeding. Doctors said she sustained severe head trauma in the crash. She also had a cast on her right arm and leg. They were both broken in the crash. She also sustained a fractured vertebrae and a punctured lung. Her chances of surviving were not good.

"There's also one more thing," the emergency room doctor told Susan and Charlie after listing off Sarah's injuries.

They both looked at the doctor.

"Sarah is pregnant. She is about 6-weeks along, according to our tests. The baby's heart rate is a little high right now, but other than that it appears to be healthy," the doctor said.

Charlie and Susan looked at each other in disbelief. Charlie began to do the math in his head and realized he and Sarah had been together six weeks prior. He wondered if she even knew she was pregnant, and if she did, why she didn't tell him. He walked towards her bed and placed his hand on her stomach. He began to cry.

"Oh, Charlie," Susan said.

She walked towards him and gave him a hug. Charlie wrapped his arms around Susan and cried into her shoulder.

"I didn't know. She didn't tell me," he said.

"Since it's so early in the pregnancy, there is a good chance she didn't know herself," the doctor interrupted.

Charlie looked at the doctor and wiped away his tears.

"What can we do? Is the baby going to be OK? Is Sarah going to be OK?" Charlie asked.

The doctor took a deep breath.

"We can keep Sarah on these machines as long as possible, but it is unclear if she will ever regain consciousness. She sustained severe head trauma and she might not wake up from that," the doctor responded. "As for the baby, the baby is doing well despite the current circumstances. As long as Sarah is hooked up to these machines, the baby is receiving the necessary nutrients to keep growing."

"So what are you saying?" Charlie asked.

"I'm saying, we can keep Sarah alive until the baby is far enough along where we can perform an emergency cesarean delivery. That would be when the baby is 24-weeks. But even then, the baby only has about a 50 percent survival rate," the doctor said.

"You can do that without Sarah's permission?" Susan asked the doctor.

"It is a controversial topic. But in special circumstances, like this, where the mother is incapacitated and unable to provide her wishes, the father of the baby is allowed to make that decision," the doctor responded.

The doctor and Susan looked at Charlie. He looked at Sarah. He had no idea what she would want. They never talked about anything like this. Neither of them ever assumed they would be in this position. All of a sudden, Charlie felt guilty for not talking to Sarah these past few weeks. The last time they spoke, he was angry with her.

"You don't have to make this decision today. You have time," the doctor said. "But we will need you to take a DNA test to verify you are the father before you make your decision."

"I understand," Charlie said, still looking at Sarah.

Charlie looked back towards the doctor.

"Do you think Sarah will ever wake up?" he asked.

"Because of the trauma to her brain, the chances of that happening are very slim," the doctor said grimly.

Charlie looked back towards Sarah. He walked towards her and took a seat by her bed. He grabbed her left hand and gave it a light squeeze. She didn't squeeze back. Her hand sat there limp. He looked up at her face. It was covered in dried blood and bruises.

"The responding officers collected Sarah's belongings that were in her car. They are in that bag by the window," the doctor told Susan, pointing to a plastic bag.

"Thank you," she responded.

"Was her cell phone in there?" Charlie asked the doctor.

"I'm not sure. We don't go through personal belongings," the doctor responded.

Charlie stood up and walked over to the bag.

"I'll be back to check on Sarah in about an hour," the doctor said before leaving the room.

Charlie opened the bag and found Sarah's cell phone. It was a little scratched up, but it still worked.

"I'm going to go make a call. There is somebody else who should be here too," he said to Susan.

She nodded at him. Charlie walked out into the hallway and paced back and forth for a moment. He went to Sarah's contacts in her phone and called Tim.

"Sarah, where are you? I've been calling you for hours," Tim said as he answered the phone.

"Tim," Charlie stated.

"Charlie?" Tim said becoming angry. "Where is Sarah and why do you have her phone?"

Charlie took a deep breath.

"Sarah was in an accident," Charlie said seriously.

"Is she OK? Were you with her? What happened?" Tim asked.

"I'm not exactly sure what happened. Her aunt called me once she found out. Sarah is in rough shape. She is unconscious and the doctor said she is in critical condition. I think you should come see her. We are at General Hospital," Charlie said.

"OK, I'm on my way," Tim said.

"Tim, there's one more thing," Charlie said hesitantly.

"What is it?" Tim asked.

"Sarah is pregnant," Charlie replied.

Tim was silent.

"It's mine," Charlie stated.

"How do you know?" Tim asked angrily.

"The doctor said she is 6-weeks along," Charlie said.

Tim was silent. Charlie figured he was doing the math in his head like he did when he found out.

"I'll see you soon," Tim said before hanging up.

Charlie had Susan add Tim's name to the visitation list. He arrived shortly after. Charlie and Susan met him in the hallway outside Sarah's room.

"You must be Tim. I'm Sarah's Aunt Susan," Susan said.

"It's nice to finally meet you. I just wish it was under better circumstances," Tim said, shaking Susan's hand.

"Me too," she said. "But I'm going to head home for the night. You two boys look after my sweet Sarah."

"We will," Charlie said, giving Susan a hug.

She left down the hallway. Charlie and Tim entered Sarah's room. Tim slowly walked towards Sarah. He closely examined her injuries before taking a seat by her bed. Charlie walked over to the window and propped himself up on the ledge.

"We were supposed to go away for the weekend," Tim said after a few minutes of silence.

"Yeah?" Charlie asked.

"I was going to tell her I love her," Tim said.

"Shit, man," Charlie said.

"Yeah," Tim responded.

"You really love her?" Charlie asked.

"I do," Tim said.

"Me too," Charlie replied.

Tim looked at Charlie. Charlie gave him a half-smile.

"You do, huh?" Tim asked.

"I do," Charlie said. "Ever since I first saw her in preschool. She has always been it for me."

"Do you think she loved you?" Tim asked.

"Yeah, but not in the same way. I always wished she did. And I guess I always thought eventually she would, but that's not the way it works, huh?" Charlie asked.

"I guess not," Tim replied.

21

Charlie and Tim took turns visiting Sarah in the hospital. Even though she wasn't conscious, neither of them wanted her to be alone. Susan stopped by once in a while to check on Sarah's progress, but she didn't visit every day like Charlie and Tim. Charlie not only tolerated Tim, but actually began to like him.

"I can see why Sarah likes you now," Charlie said one day when they were both visiting Sarah.

"Yeah?" Tim asked laughing.

"Yeah. You're a good guy, Tim," Charlie said.

"Thanks. You're a good guy too," Tim said.

"Thanks," Charlie said.

They were both sitting on either side of Sarah. It had been two weeks since she had been in the crash. She was listed in critical, but stable condition.

"In your medical opinion, all feelings aside, do you think she will ever wake up?" Charlie asked.

"It's not impossible, but it's not likely," Tim said. "Brain injuries are very hard to come back from."

Charlie frowned and looked at Sarah's face. The bruising had faded and she was starting to look like herself again. He moved his gaze to her stomach and rested his hand there. The baby was now 8-weeks along.

"What are you going to do?" Tim asked.

Charlie had taken the DNA test, which proved he was the father. But he already knew that without the test.

"I honestly don't know. I just keep hoping Sarah will wake up so I don't have to make that decision," Charlie said.

"Hypothetically speaking, if Sarah does wake up, then what?" Tim asked.

"What do you mean?" Charlie asked.

"I mean, she's my girlfriend, but she's carrying your baby. So what happens?" Tim asked.

"That's up to Sarah. Whatever she wants to do, I support her. I just want her to wake up and be able to make her own decisions," Charlie said.

"If she wakes up and wants to get an abortion, you'll support that?" Tim asked.

"If that's what she wants to do, then yes," Charlie responded. "If she wakes up, and wants to keep the baby. Will you stay with her if that's what she wants?"

Tim looked at Charlie.

"It's not my baby," Tim said.

"I know. It's mine. But if that's what Sarah wanted, if she wanted to keep the baby and stay with you, would you stay with her?" Charlie asked seriously.

"I honestly don't know," Tim answered.

"That's the difference between you and me, Tim. I'll be here for Sarah no matter what. Because if that was the scenario, and she wanted to raise my baby with you, I would let her. And I would play whatever role she wanted me to," Charlie said.

Tim looked at Charlie. He couldn't tell if Charlie was telling the truth or not, but Tim decided he was.

"Well, none of these hypotheticals matter anyways if Sarah doesn't wake up," Tim said.

Charlie took a deep breath.

"She has to wake up. This can't be the way she goes. She's too young. She still has so much to do," Charlie said.

Tim looked at Charlie again. He examined Charlie's face and could see the pain in his eyes. He knew Charlie had a deeper connection with Sarah than he did. Charlie knew what Sarah's ambitions and goals were. Tim knew what kind of food she liked and what her hobbies were, but they never talked about deep things – like what Sarah wanted for her future. Charlie probably knew those things, Tim thought to himself.

"I'm going to head out. I'll be back tomorrow," Tim said, standing up from the chair.

"Alright man, see you later," Charlie said, giving Tim a wave.

Tim turned around and walked towards the door. He stopped and faced Charlie.

"Try talking to her or playing a familiar song. The sounds might awaken part of her brain. I've seen it happen with Alzheimer's patients before, so it wouldn't hurt to try," Tim said.

Charlie smiled at Tim.

"Thanks for the tip," he said.

Tim nodded his head and walked out of the room. Charlie grabbed Sarah's hand and gave it a light squeeze like he did the day of the crash. Her hand remained limp.

"Hey Sare-bear, it's me Charlie. I don't know if you can hear me or not, but I'm hoping you can. I need you to wake up because we have a lot of things we need to talk about. For starters, you should know, if you don't already, you and I are having a baby together.

The doctors here at the hospital, that's where you are. Um, you were in a car accident two weeks ago and have been here ever since. Um, as I was saying, the doctors here had me take a DNA test and it showed I was the father of the baby you're carrying. You're about 2-months along right now, which means the baby is about the size of a raspberry. So it's still really small, but it's a fighter just like you.

Which is why I know you're going to wake up. And when you do, I want you to know I'm not mad at you anymore. I'm not mad that you didn't tell me about the baby. Maybe you didn't know, I don't know. But I'm not mad. And I'm not mad about Tim anymore either. He's been here visiting you too, and he's a good guy. I can see why you like him. He's way better than some of your former boyfriends," Charlie said.

Charlie let out a laugh thinking back on some of the losers Sarah dated. He never approved of any of Sarah's love interests. They were never good enough for her, he thought. At that moment, one of Sarah's doctors walked into the room.

"Good evening, Charlie," the doctor said.

Charlie had gotten to know the medical team taking care of Sarah since he had been visiting every day.

"Good evening, Dr. Cooper," Charlie responded. "Are there any updates on Sarah's progress?"

"We had more X-rays taken this morning. Her arm and leg injuries are responding well to the casts, so it doesn't look like we will need to do surgery. They will need to remain in the casts for several weeks still, but they should heal on their own. The fracture in Sarah's spine is not as severe as we initially thought. In another few weeks we should be able to remove her back brace. Her lung is also recovering well and should be back to normal soon," Dr. Cooper said.

"That's great news," Charlie said.

"However, the CT scans are not showing any improvement on Sarah's brain. Her brainwaves remain minimal. There hasn't been any progress on that part of her body since the crash, which makes the outlook of her waking up unlikely," Dr. Cooper said, looking at Sarah.

"But it's not impossible," Charlie said, following his gaze.

"It's not impossible, no. But I have never seen a patient recover from head trauma this severe," Dr. Cooper said, looking back at Charlie.

Charlie looked at the doctor.

"I'm just being honest with you, Charlie. I don't want you to get your hopes up for something that may never happen," Dr. Cooper said.

"I'm not giving up on her, doc," Charlie said.

"I respect your dedication. I really do," Dr. Cooper said.

Charlie looked back at Sarah.

"As for my other patient," Dr. Cooper began.

Charlie looked at the doctor confused.

"The baby," Dr. Cooper clarified, reading Charlie's face.

"Oh," Charlie said, looking at Sarah's stomach.

"Since you are the biological father, the baby is able to be covered under your medical benefits from the VA. Sarah, on the other hand, was still on her father's insurance plan. Since Mr. Simmons is now deceased, we are having a hard time getting his insurance company to work with us on covering Sarah's expenses," Dr. Cooper said.

"What does that mean?" Charlie asked, looking back at the doctor.

"Mr. Simmons' insurance agency is refusing to pay for Sarah's medical bills. But since she is carrying a child and that child is covered under your insurance plan, some of Sarah's treatments will be covered under that plan as well. Essentially, the machines that are keeping Sarah alive are also keeping the baby alive and allowing it to receive the necessary nutrients to keep growing. So that will be covered," the doctor said.

"What isn't covered?" Charlie asked.

"If Sarah stays in the state she is in right now, meaning her condition doesn't deteriorate or get better, there won't be any additional expenses. If her condition gets worse and she requires surgery, your insurance may not cover that as being vital to the baby's well-being," Dr. Cooper responded.

"And if she gets better?" Charlie asked.

"If Sarah's condition improves, she will likely have a very long recovery process that could include lengthy rehabilitation treatments, lots of CT scans and X-rays, and several doctor visits. None of which would be covered by your insurance. But we will cross that road if we get there," Dr. Cooper said.

"So let me just make sure I understand this correctly. As long as I decide to keep the baby alive until it can be delivered, Sarah can stay alive?" Charlie asked.

"In a way, yes," the doctor answered.

Charlie nodded his head at Dr. Cooper to let him know he understood.

"A nurse will be around later this evening to check on Sarah's vitals. If you have any questions or need anything in the meantime, just press the call button," Dr. Cooper said.

"OK. Thanks, doc," Charlie responded.

Dr. Cooper walked out of the room. Charlie grabbed Sarah's hand again.

"I don't know if you heard all of that Sare-bear, but I'm going to take care of you. I'm not going to let them take you off of these machines. I know you're going to get better. Your physical injuries are already healing. We just need to get your brain on the same page," he said.

Charlie replayed his conversation with Dr. Cooper in his head. Then Tim's voice echoed in his head, *play a familiar song.* Charlie's eyes widened. He quickly pulled out his cell phone and played Mariah Carey's "We Belong Together." He held Sarah's hand and sang the chorus to her as she laid unconscious in her hospital bed.

The song was almost over when Charlie felt a light squeeze on his hand. He looked down and Sarah was grabbing his hand. He looked up at her face, but her eyes remained closed. He squeezed her hand and she squeezed back. Tears started falling down his face.

"Sarah? Can you hear me?" he asked.

Sarah squeezed his hand again.

"Oh my God, Sarah," Charlie said, leaning down and kissing her hand. "I knew you would pull through. Everything is going to be OK, Sare-bear. I am here with you. We are going to get through this."

Charlie pressed the call button near Sarah's bed. A nurse walked into the room a few minutes later. He smiled at the nurse.

"She's alert," Charlie practically shouted with excitement.

The nurse looked at Sarah who was laying on the bed with her eyes closed.

"Um, Charlie, her eyes are still closed," the nurse responded.

"I know, but she is alert. She can hear me," Charlie said. "She grabbed my hand."

The nurse looked at Charlie sympathetically.

"That was probably just nerve endings firing off," the nurse responded.

"No, watch," Charlie said.

Charlie grabbed Sarah's hand.

"Sarah, if you can hear me, squeeze my hand," he said.

Sarah squeezed his hand. The nurse tilted her head and walked closer.

"Ask her another question," the nurse said.

"Sarah, can you open your eyes? Squeeze once for no and twice for yes," Charlie said.

Sarah squeezed his hand once.

"Sarah, can you hear me?" the nurse asked.

Sarah squeezed Charlie's hand twice.

"See? I told you," Charlie said with a grin.

The nurse lifted the blanket off of Sarah's legs to reveal her feet.

"Sarah, can you try to move your toes for me?" the nurse asked.

After a few seconds, Sarah's toes wiggled on both of her feet.

"Oh my gosh," the nurse said. "I'm going to go get Dr. Cooper. I'll be right back."

The nurse left the room. Charlie kissed Sarah's hand again.

"I am so proud of you, Sare-bear," he said.

Dr. Cooper and the nurse returned to the room. Charlie smiled at them.

"I knew she would pull through, doc," Charlie said.

"Do you mind if I try?" Dr. Cooper asked Charlie.

"No, go ahead," Charlie said, letting go of Sarah's hand.

Dr. Cooper grabbed her hand.

"Sarah, if you can hear me, grab my hand," he said.

Sarah grabbed his hand. Dr. Cooper's eyes widened.

"Can you wiggle your toes for me?" the doctor asked.

Sarah wiggled her toes again.

"See? She's here," Charlie exclaimed.

The doctor ignored Charlie for a moment.

"Sarah, do you know where you are? Squeeze once for no, twice for yes," Dr. Cooper said.

Sarah squeezed his hand once.

"You are in the hospital. You were in a car accident a few weeks ago. Squeeze my hand twice if you understand," Dr. Cooper said.

She squeezed his hand twice.

"Sarah, I need you to try to open your eyes for me. Can you try to do that for me? Squeeze once for no, twice for yes," Dr. Cooper said.

Sarah squeezed his hand twice. They all looked at Sarah's face. Nothing.

"Did you try? Squeeze once for no, twice for yes," the doctor said.

Sarah squeezed his hand twice again.

"Do you mind if I ask you a few more questions? Squeeze once for no, twice for yes," Dr. Cooper said.

Sarah squeezed his hand once.

"Do you know you're pregnant? Once for no, twice for yes," he asked.

There was a short pause. Then Sarah squeezed his hand twice. Dr. Cooper looked at Charlie.

"I told her," Charlie said.

Dr. Cooper looked back at Sarah.

"Did you know you were pregnant before the crash? Once for no, twice for yes," the doctor said.

Sarah squeezed his hand twice again. Charlie's mouth dropped and he looked at Sarah. He wondered how long she knew and why she didn't tell him.

"Are you in any pain? Once for no, twice for yes," Dr. Cooper said.

Sarah squeezed his hand twice.

"OK, Sarah. I want to evaluate your pain level so we can treat it if necessary. I want you to squeeze my hand once if you're in a lot of pain, twice if it's uncomfortable and you would like us to manage it, or three times if it's tolerable," the doctor said.

Sarah squeezed his hand once, twice, and then a third time. Charlie let out a sigh of relief.

"This is amazing," Dr. Cooper said, looking at the nurse and then at Charlie. "What did you do to get her to respond?"

"I played her our special song," Charlie said smiling.

"It must really be special to bring her back like this," Dr. Cooper said.

"It is," Charlie said, looking at Sarah's face.

"Sarah, I am going to let you rest for the night. I'll be back in the morning to ask you some more questions, OK?" the doctor asked.

Sarah squeezed his hand twice to acknowledge she understood. Dr. Cooper let go of her hand. He and the nurse walked towards the door, but he turned around to face Charlie.

"Good work, Charlie," he said, smiling at him.

Charlie smiled back. Dr. Cooper and the nurse exited the room. Charlie grabbed Sarah's hand again.

"Sarah, do you know who I am? Squeeze once for no, twice for yes," Charlie said.

Sarah squeezed his hand twice. Charlie smiled. He paused for a moment.

"Do you want to keep our baby?" he asked.

She squeezed his hand twice again. His heart fluttered. He felt relief. Charlie leaned down and kissed Sarah's hand.

"Do you love me?" he asked.

There was a pause. Charlie looked up at Sarah's face and then back to her hand in his. She squeezed it twice. He smiled.

"I love you too, Sare-bear. I always will," he said.

22

Two weeks after Sarah responded by grabbing Charlie's hand, she woke up from her coma state. Tim and Charlie were both next to her hospital bed when she opened her eyes. They were talking to each other about football and didn't notice Sarah was awake. She looked at Charlie and then at Tim.

Charlie thought he saw Sarah move out of the corner of his eye, so he turned and looked at her face. His mouth dropped slightly. Tim followed his gaze and saw Sarah's eyes were open. He gently grabbed her hand. Sarah slowly moved her eyes from Tim to Charlie.

"Good morning, Sare-bear," Charlie said, smiling at her.

"Yeah, uh, good morning," Tim said.

Charlie held Sarah's other hand and lightly stroked the back of it with his thumb. She gave his hand a light squeeze.

"Can you open your mouth? Can you try to talk?" Tim asked.

Sarah looked back at Tim. After a moment, her bottom lip lowered slightly. Then her lips pressed back together. She tried to open her mouth again, but she couldn't fully lower her lip.

"It's OK, Sare-bear. This is going to take some time and you've already made great progress," Charlie said.

Sarah looked at Charlie.

"Yeah, babe. You've been doing great," Tim said.

Charlie looked at Tim. He didn't like him calling Sarah babe. But they were dating before she got in the crash. Charlie didn't know what that meant for him or their baby, but he knew he wasn't going to leave Sarah's side unless she asked him to. Charlie looked back at Sarah. She was looking around the room.

"This is your hospital room," he said. "You've been here about a month now."

Sarah looked down at her stomach, which was starting to show. Charlie followed her gaze. He placed her hand on her stomach.

"Our baby is doing great. He or she is 10-weeks now," Charlie said.

Sarah looked up at Charlie. He smiled at her. She moved her gaze to Tim. Tim gave her hand a light squeeze and gave her a half-smile.

"It's OK. We'll figure it out," Tim said.

Charlie briefly glared at Tim. He was starting to not like him anymore. He quickly straightened his face out and looked back at Sarah. She was looking at the door.

"Do you want to see your doctor?" Charlie asked.

Sarah looked at him. She moved her eyes up and down.

"OK, I'll call him in here. One second," Charlie said.

Charlie let go of her hand and pressed the call button near Sarah's bed. He grabbed her hand again. Sarah looked at Charlie, then at Tim, and back to Charlie.

"Don't worry. We've been playing nice," Charlie said jokingly.

Sarah shifted her gaze back to Tim.

"We have," he said. "We both care about you and want the best for you."

Their conversation was interrupted when a nurse entered the room. She walked towards the bed and noticed Sarah was alert.

"Hello, Sarah. We've been waiting for you. How are you feeling?" the nurse asked.

"She can't talk yet, but she opened her eyes about 10 minutes ago and is aware of her surroundings," Tim said.

"That's great. Let me go get Dr. Cooper," the nurse responded.

The nurse left the room. Dr. Cooper entered shortly after. He walked towards the foot of Sarah's bed.

"Hi there, Sarah. You have quite the support team here. These two men have been here nearly every day with you," Dr. Cooper said.

Sarah's lips turned into a slight smile.

"You're regaining motion in your face. That's great! Can you open your mouth for me?" Dr. Cooper asked.

Sarah lowered her bottom lip slightly further than she did before.

"It's OK. Take your time," the doctor said.

Sarah paused for a moment and then opened her mouth a little more.

"Now, I want you to try to speak," Dr. Cooper said.

Charlie and Tim were watching Sarah intently. She closed her mouth and opened it again. A quiet sound came out, but it wasn't a word. She closed her mouth and tried again.

"Hello," Sarah said raspily.

The room let out a cheer. Charlie quickly wiped a tear from his eye. He had waited so long to hear Sarah's voice again. He smiled at her with the biggest grin. She smiled back at him. Sarah turned her attention towards Tim. Her smile swiftly faded.

"Hi," she said to him.

"Hi," he said smiling.

"Sarah," Dr. Cooper interrupted. "Do you mind if we take you back to run some tests now that you're awake?"

"That's fine," Sarah responded slowly.

Charlie gave her hand a light squeeze before he released it. Then two nurses walked into the room and wheeled Sarah's bed out into the hallway. Dr. Cooper followed. Tim and Charlie stayed in the now-empty room.

"Wow," Tim said.

Charlie looked at him confused.

"What?" he asked.

"I wasn't expecting her to wake up," Tim answered.

"I knew she would," Charlie said smugly.

"Don't get me wrong, I'm happy she is awake. Ecstatic even. I just wasn't expecting it," Tim said.

Charlie looked at Tim. He looked back at Charlie.

"So what do you think is going to happen now?" Tim asked after a moment of silence.

"What do you mean?" Charlie replied.

"Now that Sarah is awake. What do you think she is going to do about the baby?" Tim asked.

"She's going to keep it," Charlie said.

"How do you know?" Tim asked.

"Because she told me," Charlie replied.

Tim looked at him confused.

"I asked her if she wanted to keep the baby and she squeezed my hand twice, which meant yes," Charlie said annoyed.

"We don't know if she was fully alert when she did that," Tim said.

"She was," Charlie responded.

Tim raised one of his eyebrows at Charlie. Charlie ignored him and looked towards the door. He heard a bed being wheeled down the hall. About a minute later, the two nurses wheeled Sarah back into the room. She was still awake.

"Dr. Cooper will be in shortly to discuss the results," one of the nurses said before they left the room.

Charlie and Tim both looked at Sarah.

"Hi," she said, looking at both of them.

"Hi," Charlie and Tim said in unison.

There was a moment of silence. Charlie and Tim had waited weeks for Sarah to wake up. Now that she was awake, neither of them knew what to say. She looked back and forth between the two of them a few times.

"I feel like I have so much to say to both of you, but I don't know where to begin. And Dr. Cooper wants me to take it easy," Sarah said slowly, taking breaths in-between words.

Charlie grabbed Sarah's hand.

"It's OK. Whenever you're ready to talk, I'll be here," Charlie said.

"Me too," Tim said, grabbing her other hand.

Sarah smiled at the two of them. Then Dr. Cooper walked into the room. The three of them looked up towards him.

"The CT scans show tremendous improvement with Sarah's brainwaves. With these latest results, I believe Sarah will make a full recovery with minimal lasting effects," Dr. Cooper said.

Charlie, Sarah, and Tim let out a sigh of relief.

"However, she will need extensive therapy that will likely last months. Not to mention, her other injuries that are still healing and will require follow-up appointments," Dr. Cooper said.

"But you said you expect her to recover," Charlie said, looking at the doctor.

"I do, but she no longer has health insurance and these treatments will not be covered by your insurance, Charlie," Dr. Cooper said.

Sarah looked at the doctor confused.

"Your father's health insurance company is refusing to cover you since he died. Some of your treatments up to this point have been covered under Charlie's insurance since he was able to put the baby on his plan. But anything that doesn't directly pertain to the health of the baby cannot be covered," Dr. Cooper clarified.

Sarah looked at Charlie. He gave her a half-smile.

"I'll give you all some time to talk things over, but we will need to discharge Sarah at some point if she doesn't get health insurance," the doctor said.

"I understand," Sarah said.

Dr. Cooper gave Sarah a grim smile before he left the room. Sarah turned her attention back to Charlie.

"You did that for me?" Sarah asked.

"No," Charlie said, placing his hand on her stomach. "I did that for us and our growing family."

Sarah smiled at Charlie. Tim cleared his throat. Sarah and Charlie looked at him.

"Um, I think I'm going to go," he said.

"Are you sure?" Sarah asked.

"Yeah. You and Charlie have some things you should talk about. I'll be back tomorrow," Tim replied.

"OK," Sarah said, giving him a smile.

Tim leaned down and kissed Sarah on the forehead.

"Bye, Charlie," he said as he walked out of the room.

Charlie waved after him. Then turned back towards Sarah. He gave her hand a light squeeze. She smiled at him.

"You saved my life," she said.

A tear started to fall from one of Charlie's eyes. He quickly wiped it away.

"I did what I had to," he said.

"You didn't have to do anything," Sarah replied.

"I can't live in a world without you, Sare-bear," Charlie said.

Sarah gave Charlie a half-smile. Then she looked down at her stomach.

"What are we going to do?" she asked.

"What do you mean?" Charlie asked.

"About everything. I don't have insurance. What's going to happen to me? To the baby, our baby?" Sarah asked.

Charlie was silent for a moment.

"Marry me," he said.

"What?" Sarah asked surprised.

"Marry me," Charlie said again.

"Charlie, you don't have to do that," she said.

"I know I don't have to. I want to. I've always wanted to," Charlie said.

Sarah looked at Charlie seriously. He pushed his chair back and got down on one knee. He placed her hand in both of his.

"Sarah Simmons, I have loved you from the day I first laid eyes on you. You are my best friend, my confidant, and quite frankly, the best lover I have ever had. Will you make me the happiest man on earth and be my wife?" he asked.

Sarah examined Charlie's face. His forest green eyes stared at her softly. She looked down towards her growing baby bump. Then she looked back at Charlie's face. She smiled at him.

"I will," she said.

Brianna Owczarzak

ABOUT THE AUTHOR

Brianna Owczarzak is a digital journalist and author of *Tangled Love*. She is a wife, daughter, sister, niece, aunt, and most importantly – the mother to her goldendoodle, Edgar Allan Paw. Brianna has a B.S. in journalism from Central Michigan University and an AAA from Delta College. Aside from writing, Brianna enjoys hanging out with her very large extended family and binge-watching the latest TV shows. She lives in Michigan with her husband and their dog.

Made in the USA
Monee, IL
06 August 2020